EGOMANIAC

Elvis Slaughter

ISBN: 978-0-9965932-4-3

Library of Congress Control Number: 2016915844

CONTENTS

INTRODUCTION

Cut Bank is a sleepy town, seemingly without much strife, but under the bucolic surface its denizens are mired in a game of business and politics. Mary Ellen, a former realtor and social worker, doesn't know how to take no for an answer or forget who dares to do so. Phil Gravy, a lawyer who gets debarred, is Mary's ex-lover with an equally dark side. With the support of her cronies, Mary Ellen isn't afraid to use social media for her nefarious schemes and malign adversaries or show remorse in cutting ties with friends. *Egomaniac* tells the saga of Mary's actions that lead to her death, including relatives. In her latest ploy to destroy Mayor Roy Travis, who once refused to sell her real estate, Mary Ellen finally meets her match.

PART 1: SUE

CHAPTER 1

Sue was such a nice lady.

—Casey

Was it right, or was it left? Why do they name the streets like this? Why can't they just put up an arrow that tells me the way to my house?

Casey stood at the corner of Elm and Ash, scratching her head and trying to recall which street named after a stately tree she had never seen, was the street on which she lived. Daylight was fading, and she hugged her flannel shirt around her. Fall was coming early, and the air was crisp. She looked down Elm as far as she could, and then Ash. On Ash, a yard several houses down contained mountains of fallen leaves, gathered into piles, and five young children laughed loudly, their childlike giggles echoed around her, and she remembered.

Mr. Pastel and his rowdy kids. Yes, that's the road I live on.

Then, her destination sorted, she had another thought, equally disturbing. *Did I turn off the stove? Is the chowder burning right now?*

Fall in Cut Bank meant chowder and lots of it. Farmers from the eastern side of the state brought in the last of the summer's corn harvest, and the farmers' markets filled the air with scents of roasted cobs and green chili peppers. On the western side, the coastal side, the fishermen brought in crabs, shrimp, and cod, calling out their reentry at the port with the loud, guffawing voices of men excited to be land-bound again.

As Casey's mother and grandmother had, she gathered the ingredients for northwestern-style chowder early on a Saturday morning, and a kettle-full of the rich, creamy stoup (half stew, half soup) was ready in time for a late lunch. Living alone, the pot of chowder would feed her through the week, and with a full belly, she set out for an early-evening walk.

Despite getting lost on the way home, which was usual, her walk was uneventful. Crunching fallen leaves, the homey scent of wood smoke, and the jarring scratch of rakes pulling in leaves from the sidewalks filled her ears, and she was at peace. She knew every inch of Cut Bank, every family, every shop, and she had lived here as long as she remembered. If she lived elsewhere before, she didn't remember it.

Then again, she sometimes forgot much, so maybe she lived in some faraway place such as Arizona or Texas. She couldn't remember. She remembered the important things, though; she never forgot some things, such as the year. It was 1975, September. She knew that . . . her mother's chowder recipe, that she always wanted a dog, that cigarettes are bad for you and she didn't care, and that a car she never saw was in the neighborhood that evening.

She might not remember her address on Ash Street, but it wasn't important. She found her way home just the same, serenaded by the screams of Mr. Pastel's offspring, in time to see the car, she noticed early in the evening making another lazy circle past her house. It slowed just past her house, and then stopped at the end of the block.

It was dark, the car—a shiny, luxury, black sedan with four doors. The sedan looked out of place amid the beat-up pickup trucks and Subaru wagons with bumper stickers covering the back ends, with sayings such as, "Save Mother Earth, she's the only one we've got." It was too shiny, too rich, and driving too slowly.

Her neighbor's cat, no doubt attracted by the crab scent wafting from her open kitchen windows, waited on her porch. She invited him in, gave him a dish of cream, removed her flannel walking shirt, and settled in front of the television to catch the news.

Hours later, she awoke in the recliner and rubbed her tired eyes. Grabbing her flannel, she went outside and lit a cigarette. It was dark by then, and she had no desire to get lost again, so she stayed on her street. Mr. Pastel's children were long tucked in bed, and she peered through the darkness looking for the strange car.

As if it knew, she waited for another glimpse, it circled the block again, even more slowly this time. She watched quietly, smoking slowly and sending plumes of smoke into the chilly air. Three. Four. Five. She counted the number of times the car circled the block. By the end of her third cigarette, she thought she was up to ten, but she couldn't remember whether it might have been more than that. She lost track.

Casey was about to start the count again when the dark van pulled up outside her neighbor's house. Sue was always kind to her. When Casey's mother died, Sue brought over a carrot cake. Whenever Casey wanted to leave town to visit her sister in South Dakota for a long weekend, Sue happily agreed to bring in the mail and watch her house for her.

Sue drove a late-model Ford SUV of some type, perfect for getting Casey to the grocery store during a Cut Bank winter storm. Not having a car, Casey always noticed others' cars. She knew what everyone in town drove, and she knew the dark van that pulled up in front of Sue's house was not good news. Not good news at all! She saw the same van on the news reports—the one in the background as a reporter talked in the forefront about a murder, or a body found in the river, or the homeless person who didn't survive a night in the bitterly cold, snow-covered park.

It's the death van, she thought. *Why is the death van at Sue's house?*

She pulled her flannel more tightly around her slim shoulders and readjusted the stocking cap that held her shaggy, shoulder-length brown hair. She lit another cigarette and moved closer to her porch and off the sidewalk, where she had a better view of the death van. From the passenger side, a man emerged. She knew who it was before he even showed his face in the street lamp's pale-yellow beams.

Detective Gravy, I bet. That guy rides around in the death van, usually.

The tall figure was Detective Gravy, and he hurried into Sue's house. Several other men Casey didn't know by name followed him. She lit another cigarette and waited.

Ten. Or was it eleven? Her mind drifted to the sedan, which didn't come around the block again while she watched the death van. It bothered her. She wanted to see it once more, just so she could bring her count to an even twelve.

She peered down the block in one direction, and then the other. The dark sedan never came. She was about to walk inside, having enough cigarettes to get her through the night until her morning smoke, when a rustle on Sue's porch caught her eye.

The men from the van surrounded the stretcher, and Detective Gravy followed it, jotting notes on a little pad he pulled from his breast pocket. He looked both ways, up and down the street, but his eyes never saw Casey hiding in the porch shadows.

The stretcher was loaded into the van, and Detective Gravy got back in the passenger seat. Casey went inside and continued to watch from the window. All was quiet; all was still; the van was gone. The only strange thing she saw of her across-the-street neighbor's house was a new decoration—yellow tape covered in black letters. WARNING. POLICE INVESTIGATION. KEEP OUT.

She brushed her teeth and went to bed. She fell asleep easily but awoke sometime later in the night. The clock radio next to her bed said it was sometime after one in the morning. She thought about going out for a cigarette, but she didn't feel like bundling again, and the wind knocking against the shutters told her it was chilly outside. She lay awake for hours, wrestling with the taunt of a thought that refused to materialize into something vivid. It huddled, foggy and vague, just at the edge of consciousness and poked at her. Something wasn't right; something needed to be done. But what?

Five years ago, she lay awake similarly unable to sleep, but unable to think clearly about something important and serious on her mind. The morning after, she awoke and knew immediately what she couldn't remember in the night. She forgot to visit her mother in the hospital. Instead, she was caught up in a television game show and a frozen entrée with the bonus of a tiny dessert—a brownie, her favorite.

She didn't see her mother again after that, not alive. The hospital called that afternoon to say her mother died in the night—complications of pneumonia or some such thing—and that nagging feeling bothered her again, but she couldn't peg it.

She tired of chasing the nagging feeling around her brain and finally fell back asleep. And sure enough, just as five years ago, she awoke and knew what was wrong. Things were wrong on her block—the death van was there, and the sedan circled the block many, many times.

Detective Gravy didn't see the sedan; it didn't circle the block while he was there with the men and the stretcher. It bothered her. Detectives need information about strange things the neighbors see; she knew this from watching the evening news. Sometimes, neighbors see important things that help detectives, like the time a driver was changing his tire, and a car hit and killed him. A nosy neighbor over on Spruce Street saw the whole thing, and though the car drove off after killing a nice man, the neighbor described the whole thing to the police.

She looked at her clock radio, which read 9:00 a.m. She slept later than usual. Surely, Detective Gravy would be at the police station by then, drinking coffee and alternating doughnuts and puffs on a cigarette. Isn't that what all police officers do?

She picked up the phone and dialed the station.

"Cut Bank PD," said a cheery woman's voice. "How may I direct your call?"

"I . . . I saw a car, and I want to tell someone about it."

"Tell me your name, please, and where you live."

"I live on Ash Street. I'm Casey. The death van was near my house last night, and I saw Detective Gravy there too," Casey said, pleased she remembered her street name, though the street number wasn't something she could recall then.

"Death van? What do you mean, 'death van'? Oh, never mind. Detective Gravy, you said? Let me get him for you."

"Yes, good, thank you."

She waited on the line for the detective to pick up.

"Gravy here, how may I help?" His voice sounded tired, and Casey guessed it was likely because he was up late driving around in the death van.

"It's Casey. Sue is my neighbor. Is she OK?"

"I'm sorry, ma'am. I can't talk about an open case with the public. Private information, I'm afraid."

"But I have to tell you about the sedan. I saw it right before the death van came."

"Death van?"

"Yes, you were in the death van at my neighbor Sue's house, and you didn't see me because I was smoking in the bushes, and then I was smoking on the porch, and you didn't see me."

"Go on. Tell me about the sedan."

Casey told him what the vehicle looked like. She was pleased she remembered so many important details about it, such as the route it took around the block, the number of doors it had, and it was as shiny as coal.

Detective Gravy listened quietly. She imagined he took detailed notes for his investigation, and as she talked, her mind starting visualizing what slacks and top she would wear when the news program wanted to interview her. She decided on the paisley bell-bottomed slacks and a purple blouse when she realized it was quiet on the phone, and she had stopped talking.

"Detective Gravy? Are you . . . still there?"

"Hmmm? Oh! Yes, yes, still here. What else can you tell me about this sedan?"

"I told you everything."

"Very good. Thank you."

"Wait! Did I help? Is the sedan part of your mystery?"

"And what mystery would that be, Casey?"

"The mystery of why neighbor Sue didn't feed her cat this morning and why her paper is still on the sidewalk and why she didn't open the drapes in the living room with the big window in it and why she didn't call to see whether I want to go to the store with her this morning. That mystery."

There was a long pause.

"Casey, I appreciate the call, but I can't talk about this with you, and I need to get going."

"OK, but I wondered if I told you some important information . . . will the news like to interview me?"

"I have no idea. I have to . . ."

"Wait! Don't go!"

"Yes, Casey? Is there something more you want to tell me?"

"No, it's just, I'm out of milk, and I need to get to the store and . . . well, I was just wondering, should I call a cab, or do you think Sue will be able to bring me with her today?"

Another long pause.

"Casey, I'm sorry to tell you this, but your neighbor is deceased. That's all I can say. If you remember the make and model of the sedan, please call me right away. I'll pass everything along to the police chief, as he is the one handling this investigation. Otherwise, that it circled the block eleven times and had four doors is probably not going to help him too much. He needs more to go on than that. Call again if you remember anything specific, and if you don't, well, don't call. Good day to you."

The phone went dead.

Casey sat quietly in her kitchen and drank her coffee black. It tasted like tar, and she wished she had some milk. She was about to walk across the street and borrow some from Sue when she remembered what Detective Gravy said.

A tear rolled down her cheek. She would miss Sue. Sue was such a nice lady.

CHAPTER 2

She had a choice to stay or go; she chose to go.

—Mary Ellen

"When push came to shove, you just couldn't handle it, could you, Mama!" The sun darted behind a cloud quickly, as if in retreat from Mary Ellen's shaurp tone. "He was a nice boy, you know? And he liked me, which is more than I can say for most of the creeps in high school. We were just friends. Maybe we would have been more, but you just couldn't stand the thought of your little girl dating a black kid. What exactly got you frightened?"

Everyone knows the dead don't speak.

"I mean, we were just kids. Just kids! Maybe we would have gone to prom together, maybe we would have fallen in love and given you grandbabies someday, and dammit, Mama, maybe we just would have stayed friends and moved on. Who knows? I couldn't date him very well after you left me, not with that whole argument hanging over my head. It just didn't feel right, you know?"

Moving to a small bench, Mary Ellen sat and crossed her legs, her coat pulling away from her lap to reveal a tidy, sleek suit of brown silk and lean, muscular legs in matching brown snakeskin pumps. She folded her hands in her lap and exhaled slowly, closing her eyes briefly as if to shut out the sun, and then opened them again. As usual, there was no sun, not in the cloudy, dreary Northwest.

She made this pilgrimage once a year for twenty years and often thought how interesting it would be if she had a photo book of how she changed over the years. The first year she came, Brandon, her African-American boyfriend, held his arm around her, her eyes red and tear-streaked, as they buried her mom. They looked much too cheery in brightly colored plaid bell-bottoms, too cheery for a funeral, but things were that way in the Seventies. Once the crowds cleared, they stayed graveside and smoked their way through a pack of Camels before leaving.

The next year, Brandon wasn't with her when she went. Their fling about ended as quickly as it started, and Mary Ellen couldn't bring herself to be around the person she and her mother fought about in their last conversation. It was too painful. "You got no business dating a black man. Aren't there some nice white boys, football players or something? What, your kind isn't good enough for you?" Her mother's words still stung twenty years later.

Few years after, Mary Ellen started to grow up, despite having to do it on her own without a mother. She visited in her high school graduation gown, then during her college years, when she was secretly glad her mother couldn't see her. She would have had much to say about the hemlines that kept getting shorter. She and Gerald had come together, she in her wedding gown and he in his tuxedo, the year they wed. Several years after that, Mary Ellen brought Savanna, swaddled in pink and dozing peacefully in her stroller, so her mama could meet her first, and only, grandbaby.

There were lines around Mary Ellen's eyes now; her clothing was modest and befitting the professional she became. But no matter how her looks changed over the years, her eyes never ceased to fail her in dumping buckets of tears whenever she visited her mama. There was anger, too—anger that never seemed to subside—and always the memories she could not escape when she saw the words on her mama's gravestone:

Sue Pearson
December 1931–September 1975
Gone too soon, we wish you had stayed

As Sue's closest living relative, Mary Ellen shouldered the responsibility of funeral arrangements at the age of 16. Certainly, it aged her. Her choice of words on her mother's gravestone caused a few raised eyebrows, but Mary Ellen chose words from her heart, and in typical teenage know-it-all style, didn't give a damn what anyone thought. Her aunt, Sue's sister Willa, said, "Couldn't you have just said something about how we'll always miss her and never forget her?"

Mary Ellen replied, "She had a choice to stay or go; she chose to go. I wish she'd chosen differently. That's how I'll remember her; that's what I'm putting on her gravestone. You weren't there; you don't know what it was like." Mary Ellen and Willa hadn't spoken since, relegating their familial duties to generic, signature-only Christmas cards.

The other eyebrow that rose was that of Detective Gravy. He attended Sue's funeral, and Mary Ellen assumed it was because he was the responding officer the night she died and had some police obligation to attend. He offered her his condolences after the funeral and remarked, "I'm so sorry you had to go through all this, Mary Ellen. Chin up; things will get better for you."

Mary Ellen replied, "She put me through this, you know. I don't know whether I'll ever forgive her." When he raised his eyebrow then, she educated him. "You know, because she chose to leave me by taking the easy way out. Suicide is the ultimate selfish act."

Detective Gravy nodded and smiled. "Yes, I understand your gravestone engraving now. Her, uh, suicide. I see what you mean. She could have stayed if she'd wanted to. Why do you think she . . . uh . . . chose to leave?"

"I don't know, honestly. All I know is that we fought the night before, and it was the last time I saw her alive."

"What did you fight about?" Mary Ellen felt like kicking him in the teeth for his insensitivity. The number of mourners lining up to comfort her kept growing, and Detective Gravy wanted to stand around talking about painful things, such as their last fight.

Their last fight! It was not the first. Sue and Mary Ellen fought about everything—what Mary Ellen wore, why she dropped out of the school band, when her curfew could be later, why she wore thick purple eye shadow, and of course, their last fight was about her boyfriend Brandon.

"We fought about a boy. I wanted to date a boy she didn't like. Turns out, my mama was racist, and I never knew it until that argument. She hated the idea of me dating a black man."

"Seems a small thing—your daughter dating someone you don't like—and I'm real sorry she thought it was big enough to take her life over it," Detective Gravy replied, shuffling his weight to his other leg and bending his head, sympathetically.

"Who knows why people do what they do. All I know is my mama's gone, and there's one fewer racist in the world."

Detective Gravy nodded, then, patted her kindly on the shoulder, and left the greeting line. He walked away and immediately headed for the patrol car, and through the quietness of the cemetery, Mary Ellen heard him radioing headquarters and asking for the chief.

Truth was, she was angry with her mom for leaving her to face the world alone, but mostly, she felt guilt. She was ugly to Sue; she knew it. "I'll date whomever I choose, and you can't stop me," were her last words to her mom. Then, she slammed the house door, walked to her friend's house, and stayed there for the night.

Next day after school, she dawdled in the school library, finishing homework and chatting with friends, and then Brandon walked her home. At her street corner, he hugged her goodbye, promised to call, and walked back toward his home. They agreed there was no sense in angering Sue again by bringing Brandon home with her; they'd waited until things cooled and blew over.

Mary Ellen walked the last hundred yards to her house in silence, contemplating what to say to her mom and how to smooth things over. The house was dark and empty when she entered; the drapes in the family room were still drawn from the night before, and Mary Ellen's pulse quickened. She knew immediately something was amiss. Unwashed coffee cups and cereal bowls were stacked in the sink, the coffeepot was cold, and the cat's food bowl was empty. Her mother, a tidy housekeeper, would not have left home without putting the kitchen in order.

The cat, a rust-colored tabby, rubbed against her leg, and she fed him quickly, wondering how long he was without food. She moved back toward the bedroom, calling for her mother and becoming more disheartened by the silence around her with each step.

She walked into the bedroom then, noticing the unmade bed and her mother's clothes on the floor. *This is not right. This is unusual.* She called loudly, her pulse raced, she moved quickly from the bedroom to the master bathroom, the bathroom to the closet, and then . . .

Her screams didn't stop; they wouldn't stop for an untold time. By screaming, she somehow hoped she could erase the horror of what she saw, make it go away, make the pounding in her head stop. But no matter how long she screamed that day, or in her night-mares for years, she could not erase the image immediately burned in her mind. Her mother hung before her from a rope tied to a hook screwed into a beam at the top of her closet. Her neck was stretched at an odd angle, and her eyes were wide open.

In the aftermath of finding her mother, all the therapists told her it wasn't her fault. People chose suicide for many reasons, and the living left have to keep living and not abandon themselves to guilt and regret. "Nothing can change the outcome now," she was told too many times to count. "Take care of yourself now; let the past go; it's time to move forward," was the resounding message of therapists at Mt. Sinai Hospital.

Interestingly, Detective Gravy first suggested the hospital to Mary Ellen. Seeing her shock and panic when he arrived at her home that evening, he immediately called the hospital and had a grief counselor come. In the days after the funeral, she sank more deeply into depression.

She took solace in Mt. Sinai's sterile halls and spent hours crying and yelling at the white coat-clad therapists who supported her through her depression. There, she was a patient for six months and, during that time, she had only one visitor—Detective Gravy. He sat beside her bed for an hour each day, speaking with her when she wanted to speak, sitting quietly when she didn't want to speak. She became used to him, to his presence, so much so she forgot how much he upset her at Sue's funeral. He became her one true friend.

The sun came out from behind the clouds suddenly, blinding Mary Ellen. She fumbled in her bag for a pair of sunglasses and wondered how long she sat on the bench next to her mama's grave.

"All those months in the hospital, Mama . . . Brandon never visited me. Do you see? Do you see that you died for no reason? Brandon and I never ended up being anything, nothing! You were afraid for no good reason! Damn you! Why? Why did you leave me? All because you thought I'd end up with a black man?" Mary Ellen wiped her eyes and sniffled into a tissue she extracted from her large purse on the bench beside her. "I miss you, Mama. It's been twenty years, and I still . . . I still . . . I still miss you."

Her purse vibrated, and then from its depths, she heard the ring of her cell phone. She dug through notepads, pens, and lipsticks and gum wrappers until she reached it and answered it mid-ring without even checking the caller ID.

"This is Mary Ellen. How may I help you?"

"Hey, it's me, Dana."

"Oh, hey, how's it going? Is your daughter feeling better?"

"She is; thank you. We can catch up later; I really just called quickly to tell you of a last-minute change."

"Sure, no problem. What's up?" Mary Ellen blotted her eyes with a tissue as she listened, and stared absent-mindedly at her mother's grave. Dana was a good assistant, the best she'd had. A single mother, she juggled much in her life, but nothing in her personal life ever seemed to interfere with her ability to support Mary Ellen and the realty office she owned. She was punctual, attentive, friendly, and one of Mary Ellen's few friends.

"You're not going to like this," Dana continued. "I hope you're sitting."

"Yeah, I'm seated. Shoot."

"It's the Town Council meeting tonight . . ."

"Tonight? It's not until tomorrow night. Check your calendar again, missy. You're wrong!"

Dana was heard taking a slow, cleansing breath on the other end of the call before speaking again. "Yes, I know it's tomorrow night. That is, it was supposed to be tomorrow night. They changed it at the last minute. It's tonight at 6 p.m. in Council chambers."

"Are you kidding me? There are protocols and procedures to follow! The Council can't just change the meeting whenever they feel like it. It's open to the public, and the public has a right to fair notice on the day and time of the meeting! If anything, they should have moved it forward a day, not back a day!"

"I know. You're right, of course," said Dana.

"Well, what's the reason? Did something urgent come up?" Mary Ellen pressed. She was not in the mood for a Council meeting tonight, and she desperately needed a solid explanation why it was moved, if for no other reason than to make her feel better.

"No reason, not that I can tell. I saw the agenda, and it hasn't changed or been revised in any way . . ." Dana offered.

"Don't be dumb, Dana. Of course, it didn't change! We both know why they moved the meeting. As usual, the Council will do whatever it can to prevent me from attending the meeting, even if it means rescheduling it at the last minute and rescheduling it to a day like today, no less!" In this small town, Mary Ellen was sure that every person on the Council knew that today was the anniversary of her mom's death. "How dare they!"

"I'm sorry," Dana said, consolingly.

"Sorry, my ass! Cancel my afternoon meetings; change my dinner plans; call Gerald, and tell him I'll be home late. I'm not going to miss that Council meeting and give them the satisfaction of excluding me."

Without so much as a goodbye, Mary Ellen hung up on Dana and stomped angrily to her car, leaving her mother's grave behind her.

CHAPTER 3

So she's going to behave tonight? Or is this what a ticking time bomb looks like?

—*Mayor Roy Travis*

At 6:10 p.m., Mayor Roy Travis whacked his gavel on the Council table to call to order the Cut Bank Town Council meeting ten minutes later than the meeting was scheduled to begin. No one on the Council complained, and the Council chambers were empty, except for the mayor and the Council's few members. Cut Bank was that way—anywhere from 6:00 p.m. to 7:00pm was acceptable as a start time, depending on how quickly the small group caught up on friendly gossip.

As the gavel's sound rang through the cool, quiet chambers, reverberating against marble walls, the members still chatted with one another.

"Do you think she'll show up?" whispered Phil Gravy, the town's only lawyer and a past member of the police detective squad.

"God, I hope not. There's not enough Xanax in my self-prescribed bottle to get me through an evening of Mary Ellen's drama," replied Dr. Spence, the town's psychiatrist.

"Well, you'd better get that prescription filled at Council recess, Doc, because I have no doubt that Dana called Mary Ellen and let her know of the change. Dana's like that—always trying to keep the boss happy," replied Kris.

Having heard enough conjecture about whether Mary Ellen would or would not show up, Mayor Travis gave his gavel another solid whack on the table. "All right, all right, let's get down to business." He motioned the clerk and recorder to begin to transcribe the meeting.

"Let the minutes reflect a call to order at 6:00 p.m.," he said, eyeing the new clerk, a mousy girl of 25, daring her to argue the start time.

"First order of business," he continued, "I'd like to begin by going on record to share some personal professional news. That is, as we all know, elections are just around the corner. And I've decided to seek reelection as your mayor for a second term."

There were claps and cheers around most of the table, and Mayor Travis grinned.

"Well, that's great news, Roy," said Dr. Spence. "Expected, but still great to hear. Off the record, drinks are on me the next time we're at the club." The wink that followed was directed at Mayor Travis and Phil Gravy, and it definitely did not include Kris.

All business, Kris, a small-business owner in Cut Bank, pushed her reading glasses down the bridge of her nose with a sleek, manicured finger and eyed Mayor Travis. "Have there been any other registered candidates at this time, Mayor?"

"You mean is Mary Ellen going to try to give me another bit of trouble by running against me?" the Mayor asked.

"No, that's not what I mean. I meant what I asked—have any other candidates registered?"

"Not yet," Mayor Travis replied.

"I'd be surprised if Mary Ellen got involved again," said Dr. Spence. "In my experience, and especially given that I've known Mary Ellen since she was a teenager, even treated her as a patient as you are all aware, she is not one of the personality or fortitude to rise above a public defeat and step up to the line and try her luck a second time. No, I'd be surprised if she ever ran for mayor again."

"Clerk, please strike Dr. Spence's irrelevant, unprofessional conjecture from the record. The psychological profile of a patient has no place in public record. Thank you," Kris said perfunctorily. *It's like babysitting*, she thought.

"Moving on to the next order of business then," said Mayor Travis. "Let the record reflect that an unanimous vote in favor of a last-minute move of meeting day and time took place one week ago yesterday. All Council members approved the change."

Mayor Travis eyed the clerk, gazing at her without blinking until she recorded the information he just relayed. Dr. Spence and Phil jabbed each other in the ribs and winked conspiratorially, whereas Kris pursed her lips, crossed her legs, and studied her skirt for nonexistent pieces of lint to pick. *If by "unanimous," he means we never voted, I agree that we were unanimously not asked*, Kris thought.

The meeting proceeded routinely for a time. The town's budget was reviewed, plans for an upcoming harvest festival and parade were discussed, and updates on progress made with capital expenditure budgeting for the coming fiscal year filled an hour. There were innumerable statements by the Mayor ("let the record show, please . . ."), rib jabs and winks between Dr. Spence and Phil, and smothered sighs of frustration from Kris as the meeting progressed.

Kris received the vote of women and small-business owners throughout Cut Bank when she ran for a spot on the Town Council two years ago. It was her first term in public office, but she believed with good reason that the Council needed the voice of the underserved, and she was brave enough to try it.

Two years into her term, she learned too well how Cut Bank politics worked—you had to be a member of the Good Ol' Boys Club to have a say in anything. That Mayor Travis, Dr. Spence, and Phil Gravy, drank beers at the country club and every other night didn't help her cause to be part of a team that worked hard to speak for women and small-business owners. She was drowned out every time. She could hardly wait for her term to end.

Meanwhile, she did the best she could by making sure her friends, Dana and Mary Ellen, had the inside track on what happened in Council. Perhaps as a team, they could keep the Cut Bank power circle in check.

"And that brings us to our last order of business," said the Mayor. "We have an item we need to vote on regarding the rezoning of the historic Chateau du Monde as a residential, historic property, to a commercial property. Let the record show that the citizen making this request was invited into Council chambers and that this portion of the Council meeting is open for public debate and comment."

The clerk rose from her seat and hurried to the Council chamber doors, her heels clicking and clacking on the sleek, polished floor. She returned to her seat moments later with a tall black man of average height and modest build, wearing a pair of pressed khaki slacks and a fleece pullover, following her.

"Brandon Carmichael, thank you for speaking tonight with the Town Council," said Mayor Travis. "Please, share with us your vision for the Chateau du Monde. You have the floor."

"Thank you, Mayor. As you may be aware . . ."

Brandon was interrupted by the opening of the Council chambers' heavy wooden doors, which created a loud squeaking sound. The Mayor looked up from his legal pad where he prepared to take notes on Brandon's presentation, and his expression changed immediately from bored interest to defensive attention. He looked at Dr. Spence and then at Phil, a look of panic on his face, as if his cronies could do anything to change the direction in which this Council meeting just moved.

Swallowing hard, he said, "Mary Ellen, welcome to Council chambers. Please take a seat. The floor belongs to Brandon."

The look of disdain on Mary Ellen's face panicked him, and like a caged animal, he sat meekly and watched to see what she would do next. Would she begin to rant right away at the change of meeting date and time? Would she save it for later? Did she already take to Facebook and Twitter to complain about the change and stand on her social media pedestal to attack his abilities as mayor, as she did the last time they interacted?

Since Mary Ellen lost the mayoral election to Mayor Travis, she'd been on a rampage to discredit him at every turn. Some of Cut Bank's citizens applauded her and followed her every move on social media, desperate for the latest installment in the siege against him.

Phil suggested he use his legal skills to prepare a civil suit against Mary Ellen on the Mayor's behalf for defamation of character, but Mayor Travis wasn't ready to go that far. Dr. Spence suggested they work with the utility department and get a Prozac pump attached to her home's water pipes, just to keep her mellow and pliable. Of course, they all laughed at such a ridiculous suggestion but quickly agreed that Mary Ellen was fast becoming a problem.

The more openness the Town Council had in the community, thanks to the eyes, ears, and social media reports of Mary Ellen, the less the trio could run things their way, and they were quickly growing weary of that inconvenience.

To the Mayor's delight, Mary Ellen took a seat quietly in the Council chamber's public seating area and neatly folded her hands in her lap. *So she's going to behave tonight? Or is this what a ticking time bomb looks like?* The Mayor was unsure.

He turned his focus back to Brandon and hoped for the best.

"Uh, yeah, so, as I was saying," said Brandon, waiting for the Mayor's attention again. Mayor Travis nodded at him to continue, as he wiped a bead of sweat off his brow. "I have initiated proceedings to request rezoning of the old hotel so I can move forward with a business plan; I have to repurpose it.

"As you're all aware, the hotel has been out of business and falling apart for fifteen years. It's in grave disrepair and is fast becoming an eyesore. I work as a barista at the coffee shop downtown and, during tourist season the past few years, I continue to get the same question from people who visit our little town. That is, is there a local brewery, somewhere we can get a pint of beer and some great local food?

"The coffee craze is dying—I mean, don't get me wrong, people will always need coffee and we have great coffee in this area of the country—but the craft beer craze is the new wave. People want to bring home brewery T-shirts from their travels, they want to relax in a setting unique to the town they visit and, more than that, they appreciate a historic setting. The hotel is falling to pieces. I have saved for years, looking for the right location and wanting to start a brewery for . . . well, for forever. And I think the hotel is the perfect place.

"I'm happy to answer any questions, but honestly, the request is simple. Rezone the hotel, please?"

Brandon's comments concluded, Mayor Travis was forced to say the words he nearly couldn't stomach hearing himself say. Letting them move from his beating heart up through his throat and out from between his lips felt as daunting as saying the words that would call for his execution. Yet, he had no choice but to say them. "This matter is now open for public comment."

Wasting no time, Mary Ellen approached the Council table and politely asked for the floor. The Mayor gave it to her.

"I am a Cut Bank citizen, and please let the record show that I disagree with the Council approving this rezoning request."

"Thank you, Mary Ellen," the Mayor said dismissively, but she wouldn't be dismissed.

"I'm not finished yet, Mayor," she said. "With all due respect for Brandon's, er, Mr. Carmichael's business plan, rezoning the hotel is not in the best interest of Cut Bank's future."

With resignation, the Mayor motioned her to continue.

"It might surprise you to know this, but in the short time I had available to me today, between visiting my mother's grave and getting here to this meeting, rescheduled without proper notice to the public, I was able to pull together a petition signed by the required five hundred voting Cut Bank citizens, which I think you'll agree, will be enough to stop the rezoning of the hotel. You see, as Cut Bank's only realtor, I think big picture," Mary Ellen said, pausing for effect.

The Council members bristled at the suggestion that they, by default, did not think big picture, as Mary Ellen suggested.

"The Chateau du Monde is surrounded by established, residential neighborhoods. The increased traffic from a bar will not only create safety concerns for the families of these neighborhoods, but will also create parking difficulties for our citizens who live in this area. Additionally, the noise level from a bar smack-dab in the middle of a residential neighborhood is a concern for families. I have five hundred signatures of families who agree with me.

"I'm not saying Mr. Carmichael can't open his bar. I'm saying I'm not interested in seeing a thriving, vibrant family neighborhood taken down the tubes by a bar, driving down the property values of hard-working citizens who have owned homes in this area for years. As the mayor of this town, I expect you have already thought of those things, though, because the best interest of our citizens is your job . . ."

Mayor Travis held his head in his hands and thought carefully about how to phrase his response. Whenever Mary Ellen started talking about realty, he knew she was only inches away from exploding the umpteenth time about the time he lost her a half-million-dollar commission by backing out a land sale at the last moment when she was his realtor. She never let him forget it.

"Mary Ellen, your comments have been heard by this Council," he started to say before she interrupted him.

"Oh, well, that's a relief. It's so nice of you folk to pull your heads out of your asses long enough to listen to us little folk," she said venomously.

"Let the Mayor finish, Mary Ellen," Kris urged quietly.

"Your comments have been heard by this Council, and they will be taken into account when we begin our deliberation and voting session in one week's time," Mayor Travis said quickly, before he could be interrupted again.

"Yeah, see, that's the problem. You don't get to vote on this; the people have spoken. Detective Gravy, er, Phil, remind our dear Mayor of the city bylaws as they relate to petitions submitted by the people. Overriding the voice of a large contingency of this community is serious, serious business. Consider carefully, Mayor. I guarantee my social media followers and the news outlets will have a great time stoning you when I share this little tidbit about this week's latest corruption in Council chambers."

Mayor Travis rose from his seat, his face reddening with each second. "Stoning me? Are you threatening me, Mary Ellen?" Through clinched teeth and with clinched fists, he ended Mary Ellen's performance the same way he did whenever she attended Council meetings. He called the Council's bailiff. Tonight, it was John Gray, Cut Bank's newest addition to the police force and a blossoming detective.

"Officer Gray, please remove Mary Ellen from the court. Let the record reflect her statements were an indirect threat to the safety of the Mayor's life." With that, he smacked his gavel on the table so hard that the head broke off the handle and dismissed the Council meeting for the night.

As the Council disbanded, Mayor Travis muttered to Phil and Dr. Spence, "Is there any way to cut off her Internet access? This will be a mess when she logs in to her social media accounts this week, especially because I already signed the rezoning ordinance before this meeting and made a sizeable investment in the stock prices of the local hops farm."

CHAPTER 4

So, maybe you aren't a prude at all;
maybe you're just a hypocrite!

—*Brandon*

An hour after the Council meeting ended, Officer Gray released Mary Ellen from the courthouse. During that time, she was held in an interview room in the adjoining department and questioned by Officer Gray. On this, the fortieth anniversary of her mother's death, she was questioned in the same room in which Detective Gravy questioned her forty years before.

This was a little different, though. Tonight was different. No one had died tonight, only almost died. And in truth, though her anger was seething and her disgust for Mayor Travis was palpable, she never really threatened to hurt him. She only alluded to the fact that perhaps, because of her online constituents of social media followers, he should be warned that people would be angry with him and might want to stone him.

No one stones anyone anymore; he ought to know that! Mary Ellen rationalized.

Of course, no one else saw it that way, not the Mayor, and not Detective Gravy. So, she sat for an hour at a metal table in a metal chair and answered all his questions about the intentions behind her "stoning" statements, and then she was warned to keep her distance from the Mayor in the future.

"It was lame," she told her husband Gerald later that evening. The two relaxed at the kitchen table picking at the last few bites of a frozen entrée they shared for dinner. "I don't know where Cut Bank gets its 'detectives,' but I know one thing for sure: not one knows how to interrogate anybody. It's as if they don't have an original thought in their heads. They read these questions from a scrap of paper, jot their answers, but don't dig more deeply into anything I say. Then, they just move on to the next question. I mean, that's not an interrogator; that's a trained monkey!"

Gerald nodded his graying head and resettled his over large bottom in his seat, trying to get more comfortable in the kitchen chair that seemed to get smaller and smaller every year. "What's all this 'they' business? I thought it was just one cop, just Gray, whom you talked to tonight."

"You're right, dear. It was just Gray. I guess I was thinking back to Detective Gravy, who 'interrogated' me the same way about Mom's death."

"I guess I wouldn't call Detective Gravy an idiot. I mean, Phil went on to become a lawyer, you know?" He wished she'd finish her tirade and let him get on with his evening. He was missing a game show, and he was ready for dessert and his armchair.

"Oh, Gerald, everyone knows you don't have to be intelligent to be a lawyer; you just have to be a criminal and know enough not to get caught!"

Deciding there was little point and little value in continuing to understand exactly what set off his wife this time (wasn't there always something?), he stood, scratched his belly, and began to tidy the kitchen. The sooner he started doing his thing, the sooner she'd slip off to her office to plunk away at her keyboard the rest of the night and the sooner he'd be released to his armchair with the remote and a bowl of mint chocolate chip ice cream for company.

When you're married for thirty years, you know how to pick

your battles. With Mary Ellen, he learned long ago to let her win them all; it was easier that way, for them both.

Mary Ellen went to her office next, as Gerald suspected, with a tumbler of scotch in hand. She logged in to her social media accounts one by one and waged war on Mayor Travis. It wasn't unfounded, not in her opinion, at least. She had a hunch the citizens' petition to rezone the hotel into a brewery would go unheeded, and the good people of Cut Bank had a right to know their democratic rights weren't being served.

With her Facebook followers, she shared: "Your right to be heard is being undermined by Mayor Travis who, just this very evening, declared there would be a vote on the rezoning of the Chateau du Monde, even after a citizens' petition with more than enough signatures was presented to the City Council to voice Cut Bank's desire that this town not be turned into Sin City. Don't believe me? Call the Mayor and ask him yourself. His home number is (515) 643-1897."

To her Twitter followers, she tweeted: "Justice is not being served in #CutBank. Remember this when @MayorTravis seeks reelection."

To her Instagram followers, she shared a simple photo of a mailbox. On it was printed "1439 Center Grove Lane." Her tagline for the photo said, "Petition requests for keeping the Chateau du Monde a hotel, and not allowing it to turn into a bar maybe sent here." The address, of course, belonged to Mayor Travis.

She sat back in her chair. Detective Gray told her to stay away from the Mayor, but she assumed that meant staying out of his physical space, not out of his cyberspace. She smiled at her good work.

She didn't have a personal grudge against the man. Heck, he went to school with her daughter, and she remembered cheering for him as the quarterback who led Cut Bank High School to three consecutive football state titles. But that was long, long ago, and she thanked her stars daily that her daughter, Savanna, wasn't ever interested in dating the man. I mean, what would she do now if he were her son-in-law, for Pete's sake? Talk about hell on earth!

No, it wasn't personal; it was business. It was business when he lost her a sizeable commission by pulling out of a sale she counted on as his realtor. Her 5% commission on the sale would have set up her family, helped them pay some debt, and given her enough to significantly invest in a foster children's home she wanted to start in Cut Bank. She envisioned it as a clubhouse where foster kids spent time after school and on weekends and got the support they needed to handle the challenges in their lives.

Paige's Place, she would call it, in honor of the first foster child she worked with in her first job as a caseworker for social services. Paige's story was sad and haunted Mary Ellen since. A steady stream of sad stories such as Paige's stories eventually caused her to change careers. She couldn't go home at night and sleep well knowing foster kids were in homes where they felt afraid, where they were hungry, where they were nothing but a government paycheck, and ultimately, she left her job to do something different. That something was a much less emotionally demanding job—realty.

The worst part was that, weeks later, a colleague in the next town up the highway called to let her know that Roy Travis' property sold, which made her livid. Her colleague's commission of 3%, instead of Mary Ellen's 5%, saved Roy money, but it made an enemy of Mary Ellen for the near future. She made the Mayor her business wherever he went from that day forward, and she was good at being his constant impediment. A man who undermines his realtor to save himself money would undermine an entire town for personal gain, and someone had to keep him in check.

The steady stream of notifications from Facebook, Twitter, and Instagram from followers who appreciated the information she shared that evening told her she provided a necessary service to her civic companions. People wanted to know what went on in their Town Council, and Mary Ellen had no problem keeping them posted.

A text message came in then, and Mary Ellen pulled her attention away from her computer to check her phone. It was from Kris.

"Way to be vocal tonight, Mary. The Council needs your persistence. Good job and thanks."

Mary Ellen clinched her fists and threw back the last swallow of scotch in her tumbler before replying.

"Way to sit on your butt and not back me up tonight, Councilwoman. The town needs your support, instead you allowed me to be hauled out of there to jail. What kind of a friend do you think you are?"

Sure, it was a little long for a text message, but it had to be said. Kris was one of Mary Ellen's oldest friends, but the woman had no spine, at least in Mary Ellen's opinion. She was all for standing up for the little guy (or gal), until having to act, and then she stepped back from the plate. Mary Ellen didn't need friends like that; there was too big a battle to wage, and she needed all the help she could get from her friend on the Town Council. Kris wasn't coming through for her. Not one bit.

Mary Ellen walked to the kitchen, picking up Gerald's ice cream bowl from the floor next to the recliner where he slept on the way, and refilled her tumbler of scotch.

Enough work for one night, she thought. She tucked herself into bed with her drink and a crochet project on which she was working. Someday, she hoped Savanna would give her a grandbaby, and she would be ready with booties and blankets when the time came.

The next morning, Mary Ellen woke with a slight hangover and wished she didn't have that second scotch. She had a full day at the office and didn't want or need the inconvenience of a throbbing head, so on her way to work she stopped in at The Usual for a four-shot latte.

She was disappointed to see that Brandon was the barista on duty. But she didn't want to start the day with an argument, especially not with a longtime friend such as Brandon. They had history together neither would forget.

As she stepped to the counter to order, Brandon must have had the same intention because he could not have greeted her in a more friendly and congenial manner.

"G' morning, Mary Ellen. I was hoping I'd get to see you soon. Thanks for stopping by this morning; I'm glad you're here."

"And why is that?" she asked, somewhat suspicious.

"Oh, I just, well, I wanted to see how you're doing. I know it was a big anniversary for you this week, and I didn't want you to think I forgot." Brandon expertly maneuvered around the espresso machine, sputtering steam, frothing milk, and creating a latte Mary Ellen hoped would cure the hammering in her head.

She wasn't in the mood to talk about her mom, so she smiled and thanked him for his concern. "I'll be all right. I appreciate your remembering."

Brandon handed Mary Ellen her drink and paused, letting his hand linger on the cup a moment. She looked up at him, wondering why he wasn't handing it over.

"I also hoped you would come in so I could say something else. About last night . . ."

"The Council meeting, you mean," Mary Ellen said with a sigh. She wasn't in the mood to relive that drama.

"Yes. I just wanted to say that I've saved a long, long time for this brewery. And I know we don't see eye to eye on it, but I hoped that as an old friend of mine, you'd at least try to respect my goal of being a business owner doing something I love."

Mary Ellen bristled. "I respect it all right. I respect our little town's integrity more, Brandon. I hope you can respect my position that involves looking out for more than my self-interests. I'm trying to keep kids and families safe from being victims of a jacked-up city council, and I'm trying to keep Cut Bank from turning into a city of sin," she spouted. Turning on her heel, she walked away from the counter without giving Brandon a chance to reply.

But Brandon wasn't finished. "When did you turn into such a prude, Mary Ellen? Seems like you had no problem with beer back in the day when you couldn't wait to drive out to Lookout Mountain with me and chug a six-pack. Or don't you remember that? Even now, I happen to have seen you walk out of Chubby's Liquor just last weekend with, what was it, oh, not one, but three bottles of scotch! Don't tell me all that is for Gerald, Mary Ellen. So maybe you aren't a prude at all; maybe you're just a hypocrite!"

This week is the worst! She thought as she walked toward the door to leave the coffee shop. Brandon's words stung, but try as she might, she couldn't ignore them. She turned to face him in retort. "I'm neither a prude nor a hypocrite, Brandon. I drink, yes, and I have no children at home. I've seen too many families with small children ruined by alcohol. I used to be a caseworker, you might recall. This is not about alcohol for older, wiser, established adults. This is about not having this hotel turned into a bar in a family neighborhood where kids could get hurt and families wrecked. That's the difference."

She moved toward the door again and reached it just as two women were about to enter. They opened the door and walked in, and she held it open for them and allowed them to pass. Only then did she see that they held hands. She watched them walk toward the counter to order their coffee, arms around each other now, and heads close, discussing what to order.

Mary Ellen heaved a huge sigh of disgust and went to work. Later that night, from the comfort of her home computer, she shared her disgust with her social media followers:

"Cut Bank is going to the dogs. How much farther into sin will we fall? Last night, it was the question of the bar, and today, I realize we've slipped even further into sin. That's right, folks. Cut Bank is crawling with homosexuals. Saw them with my own eyes. Two lesbians nearly ran me over outside The Usual. All you righteous citizens out there, pray for our town, and if you want to avoid supporting sin, stay away from The Usual."

Satisfied that she significantly cut into Brandon's tip money with her social media posts, she went to check on her husband and start cooking his dinner.

CHAPTER 5

Please don't tell me it gets worse.

—Savanna

T he best part about being an interventionist for the school district
was the opportunity it gave Savanna to interact with kids and
help them through problems worse than hers. "The apple doesn't
fall far from the tree," her mom said after Savanna informed her she
was leaving teaching to focus on at-risk kids full time. Of course,
only Savanna knew how wrong that was. Though she and her
mom both felt a passion for helping kids in tough circumstances—
Mary Ellen with foster kids, Savanna with kids whose home lives
prevented them from focusing on their education—that's about as
close to the tree as Savanna's apple fell.

The chief difference between them, of the many to choose from,
was that Savanna didn't judge people. The kids she interacted with
every day needed acceptance, not judgment.

Some children came to school hungry without a solid meal since
their free, school cafeteria lunch the day before, some kids came to
school in clothes drenched in the scent of cigarettes and marijuana,
and some kids had irreparable defects in their cognitive abilities
because their mothers did drugs while pregnant with theme. Every
child she worked with had a sad story, but rather than let on that,
she felt sorry for them and she worked hard to give them the respect

they deserved and to challenge them to do their personal best every day.

Because they were weary of being treated as problem children among teachers and at home, Savanna's style of supporting them and encouraging them was very effective. They were receptive to her as a result, they learned and grew, and she took personal joy in their successes.

It was exhausting work, though, mostly emotionally. Savanna generally returned home from work a little after 6 p.m. each evening. That evening, she was later than usual because she had parent/teacher conferences at school. None of her students' parents showed up, not surprisingly. Still, she had to try.

Instead of going straight home, she stopped off and had a glass of wine with Melissa. A surgical technician at the local hospital, Melissa came into her life when they first met at a 5K run/walk fundraiser for a foundation supporting families of children born HIV-positive. In Melissa, Savanna found a friend with a quick wit and a big heart, and the two shared a passion for helping the under-served and underprivileged. They had dated for nearly a year.

Over a bottle of Chianti and tapas, Melissa held Savanna's hand and asked her the question Savanna knew would come up eventually. "When do I get to meet your family?"

It took Savanna a solid hour to explain her parents to Melissa and help her understand the need for a future meeting, but not something to which she looked forward. "My dad is great, really great," she said. "I mean, he couldn't be more easygoing and down to earth. My mom, though . . . I don't even know where to start explaining my mom to you."

"Oh, don't worry about it," Melissa said. "I get it. Not everyone is accepting, and the ones who aren't tend to be unaccepting of all kinds of things, not just homosexuality."

"You are so right. You just characterized my mom perfectly in one sentence. She's rigid, unaccepting, judgmental, and it would not matter if I were a lesbian or a lawyer or had two heads—she's the kind of person who finds issue with every single kind of person, and then holds it against them for the rest of their life. I mean, honestly, the day I come out of the closet with my mom will be the first day of World War III, you watch," Savanna said, squeezing Melissa's hand. "I'm just not ready yet. I'm sorry."

She had not expected to have that conversation that night with Melissa, but it had to come up eventually. She and Melissa had become so close and even discussed marrying. Neither was going anywhere, so understanding each other's families was part of it. Still, on top of the long school day, the wine, and the tough conversation about her mom with Melissa, it was an unusually long and trying day for Savanna.

Which is why, when she unlocked her house door and walked inside to hear the phone ringing, she almost didn't answer it. Most of her friends called her cell phone, and she wasn't even sure why she kept a landline anymore, except that it was always the number her mother tried calling first. Assuming it was her mother calling as she walked in the house, she almost ignored it. She just wasn't in the mood, but something pulled at her and prompted her to pick up.

"Hello?"

"Hi, Savanna; it's Joy."

A mixture of relief and suspicion flooded her—relief that it wasn't her mother and suspicion why one of her mother's best friends was calling.

"Hi, Joy. Is everything all right? Did something happen to Mom?"

"Well . . ."

"What is it? What happened?" Relief and suspicion gave way to panic and fear.

"Everything's fine, Savanna. Your mom is fine, as far as I know. I mean, I think she's fine, but I guess I really don't know. Sorry, I don't mean to be confusing. I just called to pass along something that happened today, because I think you should know. She came into the store this afternoon."

Joy managed the grocery store in Cut Bank. It gave her a bird's-eye view of the town because, at one point or another, every citizen had to shop for groceries.

"Oh? Go on; what happened?" Savanna asked, slipping off her shoes and settling into her favorite armchair. A sinking feeling in her gut told her this was not going to be a lighthearted, fun story.

"Mary Ellen, er, your mom came in the grocery today. I was out on the floor helping put up a new display when she came in, so I saw the whole thing myself. It's been a long time since I've seen her like this, Savanna. I'm worried."

"OK . . . I don't understand. What exactly happened?"

"Well, she came in and got a shopping cart as usual. But then, she blocked the doorway into the store with her cart while she slowly, methodically, used each of the remaining disinfecting wipes we keep next to the door to clean every square inch of her cart. No one could get out of the store, no one could get in, and she blocked the whole entry.

"A clerk came to get me, and I approached her and asked if she could move to the side a bit. She looked at me with daggers in her eyes and said it was a ridiculous suggestion because everybody knows you can't move a grocery cart without touching it, and she wasn't going to touch hers until it was perfectly clean."

"Well, I know Dad has been fighting a cold at home this week. Maybe she was just trying to take precautions to not bring home any germs," Savanna offered.

"It gets worse."

"Oh."

"She finally finished cleaning her cart, much to the relief of everyone lined up behind her and in front of her, and proceeded into the store. I followed her at a safe distance; I don't know why. I guess I just felt something wasn't right with her, and I wanted to keep a close eye.

"Anyway, she went down the aisle and stopped at the refrigerated case where we keep the eggs. She picked out a dozen and opened the lid. There must have been a cracked one in the package, because she put it back right away. The next one she opened also had a cracked egg in it. She put that one back too. And then, she picked up a third dozen, opened the lid, and that's when she lost it."

"Lost it?"

"Yeah. She threw the package on the ground, whirled, and stuck her finger in the face of the first person she saw, who happened to be Mr. Cumberland, the nicest man anyone has ever met—"

"I know! He's so sweet! So what did she do?"

"She started yelling at him! She accused him of breaking all the eggs, on purpose!"

Savanna sighed. It was happening again.

"So, I went to her and put my arms around her, you know, like a hug. And I said, 'Mary Ellen, I have some nice fresh, new eggs in the back. Come with me, and let's get you some, OK?' She followed me like a lamb, and I called for a cleanup, but poor Mr. Cumberland looked like he saw the devil himself!"

"I can imagine! That poor man! Well, I—"

"No, hold on. There's more. I got her the eggs and asked whether she needed to shop for anything else. She said no and proceeded to the checkout line. I figured she was done with whatever craziness she walked in with and went back to work. Then, it couldn't have been but a few minutes later, I heard her screaming in the soda aisle, yelling at the top of her lungs. I rushed to her, and she was sitting on the floor with her arms wrapped around her legs, like in a seated fetal position, and screaming. I went to her and asked what was wrong.

"She said a man in the aisle kept looking at her, and she didn't want him to. I asked her why, and she said she was afraid he would kidnap her and make her wear a burka. I looked up to the poor man she accused, and he just shrugged at me, as though he didn't have a foggy clue what he had done or said that set her off."

Savanna was silent, listening. This was worse than she thought. "Please don't tell me it gets worse."

"I put my arm around her and took her back to my office and got her a glass of water. She stayed there for an hour or so, just rocking quietly in my desk chair and sipping on the water. Then, suddenly, as if someone waved a magic wand and made it all disappear, she stood and asked why she was in my office. I didn't have the heart to tell her what happened, especially because whatever fog descended on her seemed to have cleared, so I just told her that we had been having a nice visit.

"She smiled, nodded, and said she had to get back to Gerald. I asked her whether she wanted me to help her and whether she needed anything besides her dozen eggs, and she just looked at me with the strangest look on her face and said, 'Eggs? I have five dozen at home already, why would I need more eggs?' Then, she just left. Just walked out, shaking her head as if I were crazy, went to her car, and drove off, as peaceful as a dove. I thought you should know, Savanna. I'm sorry."

"Sorry? Why are you sorry?"

"I don't know. I guess I'm sorry I had to tell you. I just thought someone should know, and I didn't want to worry Gerald. If you want to tell him, go ahead. Whatever you think she needs. I'm worried about her."

"I know; I am too. Well, thanks for calling to tell me. Really. Thank you. I'll check in on her tonight and give Dr. Spence a call."

After the call ended, Savanna sat in her chair for a time, thinking. Her mom's paranoia hadn't flared up in a long while, and she knew Mary Ellen took medication for it that helped.

She thought back to the last time her mom relapsed on the afternoon of her high school graduation ceremony. Mary Ellen flew off the handle when the cake was cut to reveal a chocolate center, instead of the vanilla she thought she ordered. In the middle of their garden, surrounded by friends and family gathered to celebrate Savanna's graduation, her mother launched into a tirade. She ranted about how the baker must be a Communist who thought he knew what was best for "the people" and how she wouldn't stand for

Communists moving into Cut Bank and telling her she had to have a chocolate cake, instead of a vanilla.

That same night, her mother sneaked out of bed and disappeared for three days, and no one could locate her. No one knew whether it was a coincidence, but during that time, seven black cats were found dead at various locations across Cut Bank. When her mom finally returned home, she was dirty and hungry, but she could not remember any of the scene at the party and asked why we kept her from showering.

Dr. Spence had changed her medications then, and she'd been normal since, for the past ten years. Of course, normal for Mary Ellen meant she was still homophobic and still had a propensity for raising Cain whenever the Mayor so much as took a breath, but for Mary Ellen, that was normal.

Savanna called her dad first, and when he said her mom was sleeping and asked could he talk to her tomorrow instead, she agreed. There was no point in ruining a good night's sleep for him with this troubling story, and if her mom was out for the night, Savanna figured she would stay asleep, probably.

The next call she placed was to her mom's doctor, Dr. Spence. She called the office, left a message with the on-call service, and let them know it was urgent. When she didn't hear back for fifteen minutes, she called again, and the call service assured her they paged Dr. Spence the first time. She waited. Impatiently. Dr. Spence didn't call. So, she looked up the personal cell-phone number he gave her for emergencies and called it. She got his voicemail and left a message that she needed to speak to him urgently about her mother. Then, she followed up with a text message.

Finally, an hour later, after he still didn't call back, she went to bed. Though she kept her phone next to her bed all through the night, he did not return her call.

CHAPTER 6

As usual, thank you for another productive meeting.
Now, back to building our empires and slaying dragons
and all that juicy stuff.

—Dr. Spence

"You are the first to arrive, sir. I will let the others know you are waiting once they get here." The neatly coiffed, perfunctory spa attendant at Cut Banks' country club was always a joy to Mark Crew. He appreciated those who made it their business to recognize him immediately and lavish on him all the respect deserving of the town's police chief. On the contrary, those who didn't think it important to know who he was or how he should be treated were . . . well, not worth his time.

"Thank you, Gretchen," Mark said. "If I hear from the police blotter that your brother is out after curfew getting into trouble tonight, I'll be sure to give him a gentle nudge home."

"Thank you for looking out for him, Chief. My mother and I appreciate your extra care. Now, your sauna is waiting, sir. Follow me."

The sauna was by far his favorite meeting place in all Cut Bank. For one, Gretchen always made sure it was reserved for a full hour for him, Roy, and Dr. Spence, and no one ever rudely interrupted their session. And two, he always felt certain that there was a limited opportunity for eavesdropping because, by being in the country club, this sauna already kept out 95% of Cut Banks' riffraff. The other 5% were his kind of people—the rich and influential—and they were too busy wielding their bank accounts and personal power to pay much attention to his affairs. *It's as it should be*, he thought, settling on a bamboo bench and allowing the heat to envelop him.

The door opened, and the Mayor, Roy Travis, entered, followed by Dr. Spence who insisted on being called Dr. Spence by even his closest friends. Mark looked up.

"Afternoon, gentlemen," he said. "Mayor, Doctor." He nodded to each in turn, but first to the Mayor who had a hand in making sure his budget for the police force was as it needed to be.

"How are you, Mark?" asked Roy. "Your family is well, I hope."

"Oh, yes, no issues whatsoever. Pauline has a bit of a cold this week, and you know how it can be on the home front when the wife is under the weather. But Jude and Jade have just been tiny troopers putting up with her moods."

"Ah, you have the most adorable twins. Seventeen now, aren't they?" asked Dr. Spence.

"Not far from it! Just a week or so until their birthday. That reminds me; I was thinking City Council should submit a measure to increase the legal driving age. What do you think, Mayor?" Mark chuckled. "I'm thinking Cut Bank doesn't need to see my two hooligans on the road until they're at least 30!"

Roy laughed. "Now, now, you know I would if I could—anything for my old friend. But the three of us know there's more to City Council than that—we have bigger, more important things to handle," Roy said ominously.

"Oh, and what's that?" asked Dr. Spence. "You sound like you have something important on your mind, Mayor."

"I do; I do, indeed."

"Well, have a seat, and let's get down to business then, gentlemen." Mark was intrigued.

2 3

Egomaniac

"I had a call from Willow Bend this morning," Roy began. Willow Bend was a town the same size as Cut Bank but in the next county. It wasn't unusual for professionals to practice in both counties and in other neighboring cities to flesh out their practice. Dr. Spence, for example, saw patients in Cut Bank, Willow Bend, Chestnut Grove, and Hammerling, travelling between the four towns over a month. Each town was thriving, but not big enough on its own to keep a busy professional busy, so he expanded his service area to cover all four, as did other professionals.

"From whom? Ol' Jake?" asked Dr. Spence, referring to Jacob Whistler, the mayor of Willow Bend.

"No, it was from the office of the state bar association," said Roy. "It seems our Phil Gravy is in a bit of trouble with the bar."

"What kind of trouble?" asked Mark, as his curiosity piqued.

"Well, it's all hush right now, of course," the Mayor said. All three leaned in close. "Willow Bend First Bank has filed a grievance against Phil, citing that he embezzled funds from them while preparing their corporate taxes last year, and an investigation is pending. There is enough preliminary evidence in Willow Bend County to suspend him from practicing in their city and, pending the results of the investigation, he might be looking at being disbarred altogether, statewide." The Mayor leaned back against the bamboo wall, a satisfied look on his face.

Dr. Spence and Mark looked at him thoughtfully. Momentarily, all three were silent.

Dr. Spence chimed in first. "Well, Roy, you know we've been looking for a reason to kick him off the Council, anyway. This seems as good a reason as any. So long as there's suspicion about his credentials and suspicion that they might be removed, I think we'd be doing Cut Bank's reputation and our Council a favor by vacating his Council seat."

"My thoughts exactly, Doctor," said Roy. "I've always questioned his loyalty, and he's a pain to work with. Always arguing the other side of things, you know. I like 'yes-men,' you both know that, and believe me, if I could rid our Council of Kris and Phil in one fell swoop, I'd do it in a heartbeat. I even thought about annexing part of our city limits to create a need to diminish the size of the town and decrease Council representation. I thought of everything, and this might just be our lucky day. After all, if we could whittle the Council down to the three of us, you know we could get some real work done."

"It sounds like it's settled then. The only question that remains is how we go about letting Phil know he's been ousted," said Dr. Spence.

"Hold on just a moment; I think you're both forgetting something."

"What?" Roy and Dr. Spence asked in unison.

"Think back; think long and hard. Why do we keep Phil close to us at all when he's such a cantankerous nuisance? You think we do it just for fun? You're forgetting our history with him and the reason we put him on the Council in the first place. We keep an eye on him for a reason, remember?"

Not wanting to spell it out in a place as public as a sauna, though the chances of it being bugged were next to nothing, and the Police Chief had it checked for hidden microphones once a week, Mark looked at Dr. Spence and Roy squarely in the eyes, willing them to remember. But with as many secrets and skeletons as this trio kept track of, he knew it might be challenging them to remember something that happened forty years ago. So, he intensified his glare, raising one eyebrow for emphasis, and said, "Think, think . . . think back forty years . . ."

"Oh," said Roy slowly. "The evidence."

Mark lifted his finger to his nose in a universally acknowledged sign of "Bingo, you got it!" and waited for Dr. Spence to catch on.

"Mary Ellen's mother, you're talking about," said Dr. Spence.

"Yep, bingo! I know it's difficult to remember Phil as a police detective because it seems he's been a pain-in-the-ass lawyer forever, but once upon a time, he worked for me. And there was that business with absconding and disposing of official police evidence from a crime scene I asked him to attend to, and he did. And he never said a peep, but piss him off, and that might change."

"Well, you're right. This is by no means an open-and-shut case then," Dr. Spence agreed. "I guess we could always let him stay and hope this whole disbarring business passes over. Maybe we could even "help" with the investigation, you know, as an unbiased party in a neighboring town, just to make it go away more quickly. Then, we have Phil in our back pocket for sure, and the cards would be even again."

"It's not a bad idea, Doctor, but I think you're forgetting Mary Ellen."

Dr. Spence leaned back in the sauna, whether because of the heat in the room or because of the mention of Mary Ellen wasn't clear. Few people realized it, probably even including the Mayor and the Police Chief, but he rarely forgot Mary Ellen. The woman was his nightmare. If she wasn't calling him to talk her off a proverbial ledge, and even some actual ledges in years past, she was calling with asinine questions about her medications and to tell him about her husband's symptoms or her neighbors' symptoms, to see if he thought she should encourage them to have a psychiatric evaluation.

If Mary Ellen wasn't calling, her husband or daughter was calling, concerned about this or that nonsense. Why, even today, right until the moment he changed out of his day clothes into his sweat gear, his pager was beeping from the office and the staff was leaving him a message on his phone to call Savanna. Yes, Mary Ellen was always on his mind, but in what way did anything about Phil Gravy's potential disbarring have to do with her? "The heat's getting to my head, Mayor. You'll have to be specific. What are we forgetting about Mary Ellen?"

"Let me help," said Mark, piping in. "It's that Mary Ellen is already looking for reasons to point her social media assault rifle at the Mayor and the Town Council. If she gets wind that we knowingly kept an under fire lawyer on the Council, she'll go public. Even more than that, she'll wonder why, and we don't need her poking around and asking why we kept him. Do you catch my drift, Doctor?"

"It's that, but it's another thing too," said Roy. "Remember Phil's history with Mary Ellen. According to Savanna, and she told me this herself back in high school, Phil was the only person who got her through her depression when she lost her mom. While keeping an eye on her as you requested, Chief, he fell in love with her.

"Now, I can't possibly understand that, unless she was 50 pounds lighter and seventeen shades prettier back then, with some hidden charm she's lost along the way, but the fact remains—he loved her. And people don't forget things like that. I mean, think of it this way. Yes, it's bad enough that we have Mary Ellen on our tails and tweeting all her nonsense about me every chance she gets, but she's only one person. Let on to Phil that you knew about his license issues and chose to keep him anyway, and he might start asking why! If he suspects it was to keep Mary Ellen quiet, well, he might just switch sides and start batting for the other team."

"What do you mean, bat for the other team?" Mark asked.

"He might move his loyalty to Mary Ellen, tell her all about the evidence, and turn the tables on us!" the Mayor clarified.

"It is a predicament; that's for sure," said Mark, nodding his understanding of Roy's viewpoint. "There's always a way out though, gentlemen. You know that. For men like us, men with the upper hand and a sense of destiny, we always make a way to ensure the cards fall as we expect. We just need to think on it, I believe."

They sat quietly then, in the comfortable silence in which three men can when they've conspired and plotted with one another for decades. The steam pumped into the room, bringing with it a new scent. It was Gretchen's way of letting them know their hour-long reservation of the sauna was almost up. She added a few drops of scented oil to the water that misted into the room, and the aroma enlivened them and began to pull them back to alertness.

"Leave it to Gretchen," Mark said. "That girl is amazing! I love sandalwood. Last week, it was geranium, and before that, wasn't it peppermint?"

"Oh, who cares?" Dr. Spence griped. "We have bigger issues than remembering what kind of funky hippie scent your little love child added to the water, Mark."

The heat of the steam masked his blush as he thought back to the rendezvous he had with Gretchen's mother and the extra cash he had the Mayor pad his budget with to keep her quiet about it and raise the girl. *It's too bad when you start paying them off that they no longer seem so open-minded to fooling around anymore. They'd rather have the cash. I miss that hot little number.*

"Here's what we'll do," said Roy. He had been quiet and thinking, unaffected by Dr. Spence and Mark's conversation. "It's really quite simple, gentlemen."

"Don't keep us in suspense, Roy. The steam's dissipating," said Dr. Spence.

"It's a two-part plan, really. First thing tomorrow morning, I'll call Jonas Smig." Jonas was the editor of the region's only newspaper, and its circulation covered the four-city spread that included Cut Bank, Willow Bend, Chestnut Grove, and Hammerling. As everyone knows that newspaper folk don't make much money, over the years, Jonas proved a person who could be bought. As long as he wasn't asked to print a mistruth—even journalists have scruples—and the price was right, he was willing to ignore some news stories that crossed his desk.

"Good idea, Mayor," said Mark. "Just ask him not to publish anything about the investigation into Phil's legal license or anything about the bank embezzlement. Let's just pretend we don't even know about it."

"More than that, let's keep Mary Ellen from knowing about it," Dr. Spence added. "And I can do you one better. You keep this out of the papers, Mayor, and I'll do my part on Mary Ellen. She's due for a new set of prescriptions soon, maybe even tomorrow, and I'll simply increase her dosage of antianxiety pills. She'll float through town like she's on a cloud and won't have even the slightest inkling to start causing trouble, in any forum."

"That sounds real good, Doctor. Maybe add in a muscle relaxer and a horse tranquilizer, too, while you're at it, eh? Can you do that?" the Mayor laughed.

"I'll see what I can do," the doctor said, smiling. "We don't need a body on our hands;

We just need a more controlled, passive version of Mary Ellen."

"Agreed," said Mark.

"Agreed," said Roy.

"Very well, gentlemen. As usual, thank you for another productive meeting. And now, back to building our empires and slaying dragons and all that juicy stuff," said Dr. Spence. "See you next week."

PART 2: MARY ELLEN

CHAPTER 7

After all, there was a piece of Mary Ellen he would always have with him, even if she had moved on and started a family without him.

—Phil Gravy

"Yes, I'll have another. Make it the house Cabernet this time, please," Phil said. The server smiled at him, removed his empty wineglass, and turned to pour him another. As soon as her back was turned, he allowed his eyes to linger for as long as possible on her tight rear end hugged by a short, leather skirt. *Leggings are a privilege, not a right, and I'm glad this bar understands that. The servers here are always hot. I wonder how they get around employment discrimination laws if a girl who isn't a 10 tries to apply for a job here. I should offer my services.*

The few days since the last Council meeting when Mary Ellen appeared went downhill quickly, and Phil Gravy attempted to make sense of it all the only way he knew how, by drinking heavily. There was the way Mary Ellen looked at him in the Council meeting, the way she insinuated that he was "one of them" who fell in with the Mayor's small group of swindlers and bylaws-massagers. What was it she said? "Detective Gravy, er, Phil, remind our dear Mayor of the city bylaws as they relate to petitions submitted by the people.

Overriding the voice of a large contingency of this community is serious, serious business."

It was true, what Mary Ellen said. The Mayor was on shaky ground if he thought he could override the people's petition, and she was right in saying that as the Council's legal representative, he is obligated to make sure the city's bylaws are followed. But did she have to say it so vehemently, as if she already accused him of not upholding the law and, thereby, lumping him in with the Mayor, Dr. Spence, and Mark? It's what it felt like, and the look in her eyes—daggers ready to stab him if he faltered—said it all.

She didn't always hate me; not so long ago, she loved me. If it weren't for me, she would still be in a pit of depression, most likely.

Phil thought back to the days he spent with Mary Ellen in the mental health hospital after her mother died. Undeniably, he went to her bedside under false pretenses, sent there by the Police Chief to learn what Mary Ellen remembered about her mother's death. But she was so peaceful in her bed, lying there heavily medicated, hair splayed out on the pillow, and the smile of an angel on her lips.

He couldn't believe he had not noticed her beauty before that night, around town, at the local diner, or in the frozen food section of the grocery. He'd seen her before her mother's death, but not as he did in those few days afterward. As she slept, he watched her; as he gazed at her, he fell in love; when she awoke, he couldn't leave her side. In the months after, they were inseparable.

He wondered if she remembered. The way she spoke to him in Council chambers indicated she didn't, that their history together was too long ago.

He was her first, and she cried in his arms afterward. How does a woman forget that man, the man who gently received her innocence?

The server returned with his glass of wine, and he sipped it slowly, pensively.

"You look like you're in a stew tonight," the server said.

Phil glanced up at her, saw the concern in her eyes, and smiled half-heartedly.

"I am, sort of. Hey, may I ask you something?"

The server took a step back and eyed him skeptically, one eyebrow cocked. "Uh, sure, but before you do, you should know I don't date customers."

Phil laughed. "Oh, no, I wasn't going to ask you out. Not that I wouldn't, because you seem like a beautiful and caring person, but I respect that boundary with customers and . . ."

"What were you going to ask, then?" the server interrupted his rambling attempt to extract himself from the hole he was digging.

"Oh, I was just going to ask if you remembered your first . . . you know—the first person ever you were with—"

"Sure, I do," she said wistfully. "That's one of those things you never forget. But we're different people now, you know? I see him around town, but it's not the same. We've both changed a lot over the years, and that's just the way it works. We were together for a season of our lives, not meant forever," she said, before being distracted by another customer taking a seat at the bar. "I hope that helps," she said and winked at Phil before walking away.

A season, he thought. I liked her better in spring, and this winter we're in now is cold and bitter.

She wasn't the person he remembered forty years ago. Mary Ellen was vicious now, aggressive, and vindictive. He was well aware of the social media war she waged against the Mayor. The man could barely belch without it being blasted all over the Internet and twisted into something unnatural and vile. And Phil understood the motivation behind it—the Mayor cost Mary Ellen a fortune in lost revenue, and some things are difficult to forgive and forget.

But what did Phil do to Mary Ellen? He was always kind to her, from the first time they met. He was her support system when her mother died, and he even did what he could to exonerate her name as a suspect in her mom's death. Wasn't that worth something?

The more he thought about Mary Ellen and all he had done for her over the years, the angrier he became. When his wineglass was empty, he ordered whiskey, instead.

I'll set her straight, let her know I don't deserve to be treated that way, not in public and especially not in Council chambers.

He worked his way through a quarter of a bottle of Jack Daniels, one shot at a time, while he contemplated the smear campaign he could launch against Mary Ellen. By the time he finished plotting his offense against her, he believed he had a solid plan to get even for her suggestion that he was anything but an upstanding citizen and lawyer. The sooner he put his plan into action, the better. It would only be a matter of time before Cut Bank learned what was happening in Willow Bend, and he needed to act fast. The best defense is a solid offense.

In high school, Phil was the state wrestling champion as a freshman and the three years after. He knew how to grapple, and he knew people's pressure points. He was certain that if he started on Mary Ellen's reputation, he could have it pinned to the floor and have her squealing for mercy by week's end. Although he wasn't sure what dirt he would dig up and make public, the cornerstone would be something to the effect of what a hypocrite she was.

Does the town know that she is a functional alcoholic, despite her crusades to keep bars and breweries out of residential neighborhoods? Does the town know she lives on antianxiety medications, despite her public persona as a strong pillar of the community and advocate for citizen rights? Does the town know her daughter Savanna is a lesbian, despite how vocal Mary Ellen is about homosexuality being the devil's work? No, he doubted the town knows about any of that, and he doubted Mary Ellen even knows about Savanna.

Feeling solid in his plans to teach Mary Ellen a lesson finally, he decided to switch to beer to wind down his night. *A few light beers and I'll head out*, he thought.

He looked up at the television above the bar and watched with one eye on the screen and the other on the plunging neckline of the hot server standing nearby. It was one of those true crime shows—

the kind where some overzealous female tries to educate her viewers why the husband suspected in his wife's murder is the one who did it and the biggest lowlife scumbag ever. "He took away her car keys, folks. He wouldn't even let this woman drive their kids to school, he was *that* controlling. I mean, what a prick, right? Then, a month before he murdered her, folks, he took out a life insurance policy on her. A big one, folks. He took out a life insurance policy, started controlling every aspect of her life, wouldn't let her see her friends, and then murdered her . . ."

"Shit," Phil said.

The server glanced at him, assuming he was aghast at the husband's callousness, as she was—but he wasn't aghast. Rather, he was watching his plan of attack against Mary Ellen fall apart like a house of cards, tumbling in an instant.

"People forget that as soon as someone dies under mysterious circumstances, everyone suddenly remembers how the husband or the boyfriend or the ex-lover treated them before they died. Nine times out of ten, it's led up to the death that makes all the difference in the case. Their behavior beforehand makes a bigger difference than anything found at the crime scene," the server said.

Phil just nodded.

"I watch these shows all the time," she added to explain her views.

He nodded again, trying to look calm and agreeable. Inside, he was reeling.

Phil's house was on the outskirts of town. He liked the quiet of the countryside after a long day of work, and he didn't enjoy neighbors. He found a place years ago that he loved—a decent-sized house on 10 acres of wooded property. He remembered thinking then that if the forest caught fire, his house wouldn't survive. It was too close to the tree line, and he liked it that way—quiet, secluded, peaceful. So, he did not cut one tree and, instead, purchased a firesafe vault for his valuables and belongings he didn't want to see lost to a fire. In that vault was a file called *Mary Ellen*. In the file was a document he worked hard to create, naming him the primary beneficiary of her estate in the event of her death.

Mary Ellen's mother was left a large fortune when her father died. He was a real estate tycoon back East. She lived simply and inexpensively, and her money was well invested, and it grew substantially during her last years. When she died, Mary Ellen received a stock portfolio worth several millions of dollars. Phil knew this because they dated when the will of Mary Ellen's mother was read.

Years later, after Phil and Mary Ellen broke up, she came to him for legal advice on estate planning. She and Gerald were married by then with two children, and it seemed to her then that documenting her estate's value and creating a stronger investment portfolio was the responsible thing to do. Phil was still single then, nursing a broken heart and a fair amount of anger at the way things ended so angrily between Mary Ellen and him. He still recalled how jealous he felt when she and Gerald walked into his new law office and asked for his help, especially because he still struggled to pay off law school.

But, as a favor between old friends, as Mary Ellen put it, he helped with her estate planning. He smiled as he listened to her detail what she knew of her wealth. He smiled as Gerald held her hand and gently said, "And don't forget about the properties in New Hampshire your mom left to you, dear." He smiled as he prepared her documents and took great care to dot every "i" and cross every "t."

He smiled even bigger when he presented the documents to Mary Ellen and walked her through all the places she needed to sign to legitimize them. And he celebrated with an expensive bottle of champagne when he tucked the statement of beneficiary identification into his safe, a document he slipped into the stack and had her sign without realizing it. "It's just a document that says that when you die, my law office is designated as the executors of your will and disposal of your estate," he explained to her.

After that day, he found it easier to move on and begin to date again. He would always have a piece of Mary Ellen with him, even if she moved on and started a family without him.

Of course, this now presented a problem. In the event Mary Ellen died, just as the husband on the true crime show, he needed to be perceived as someone who was her unwavering friend for her entire life. He needed people to look at him and think that he never stopped loving her, that she was his first love and last love, and that somehow she wanted to reward him for that by leaving her estate to him. Cut Bank needed to know that Phil Gravy. A smear campaign against Mary Ellen now could spell big trouble for him in the future.

More than that, he needed to be perceived as a family friend. As much as he couldn't stand the overweight pansy of a man Gerald was, he needed people to think they were friends.

The smear campaign was off. He would just have to suck it up and deal with Mary Ellen's cutting remarks and her public disdain when she learned he was about to be disbarred. It would be worth it in the end, one day, when she made him a millionaire overnight.

Phil stood from the bar, stretched, swallowed a last swig of beer, and paid his tab. While he waited for the server to run his card, he made a call from his cell phone, making sure to speak loudly enough for everyone in the bar to hear him.

"Good evening, Gerald. How are things? Just thought I'd call and check in and see how you and the family are doing," he said.

CHAPTER 8

People always think the husband did it for insurance money, when in actuality, no one really ever knows what it's like to live with some women.

—Gerald

Gerald hated when the phone rang in the evening, especially when Mary Ellen wasn't around to answer it. He worked hard all day as an administrative assistant for the Cut Bank Independent School District, and his evening routine was his retreat from crowded school hallways, noisy kids, and a demanding principal. No one called him; anyway, it was always either a telemarketer or a call from one of Mary Ellen's friends. Savanna didn't call home much, and usually, she only called to speak to her mother. He had few friends, and most he just caught up with at the pancake house on Saturday mornings because phone conversations weren't their thing.

That evening in particular, he needed time to unwind. Standardized testing week for the school district meant an unusually large call volume from parents keeping their kids at home to protest standardized testing, and the excuses they gave for their kids' absence were annoying. Why couldn't parents just be straight about it, instead of creating dentist appointments, mysterious stomach illnesses that lasted precisely five days, and an uncanny number of sprained ankles? Gerald was good at seeing through bullshit, and that evening, he needed to unwind and detox himself from having nearly drowned in it that day.

He was watching one of those shows about a murdered woman, and the husband seemed a likely candidate. The woman hosting the show made sure her viewers knew how guilty the husband seemed, and Gerald wasn't buying it. People always think the husband did it for insurance money, when in actuality, no one really ever knows what it's like to live with some women. Some women are especially difficult.

He had a beer, and he had just settled into his favorite recliner when the phone rang. Not expecting any calls that evening, he did not bring the cordless phone with him to the recliner, and he hated that he had to get up, find the remote, mute the volume, and go into the kitchen to answer it. He did it, anyway, because Gerald always did the right thing.

Sighing, he heaved himself out of his chair and walked toward the kitchen. He rationalized that it wasn't too big of an inconvenience because he would reward himself for the effort by bringing the cookie tin back to his recliner with him once he dealt with the phone call, and that somehow made the whole business seem much more worthwhile.

He looked at the caller ID before picking up—Phil Gravy. His bullshit meter registered in the red. *That guy never calls unless there's something in it for him.*

"Hello?"

"Good evening, Gerald. How are things? Just thought I'd call and check in and see how you and the family are doing."

"Oh, hello, Phil," Gerald said, feigning surprise. "Always nice to hear from you. How are you?"

"Oh, just fine, just fine. I know this is a tough week for Mary Ellen, you know with the anniversary of her mom's death and all, and I just wondered how she's doing."

It was always a tough week for Mary Ellen, always some drama going on, but this week was always most difficult . . . and it had been that way for forty years.

"Uh, well, she seems OK. You know, just her usual, I guess. She's out now. Otherwise, I'd hand the phone over. She seems fine, maybe a little moodier than usual."

"Well, I'm glad to hear it."

"She seems a little more prone to annoyance this week, but I don't know if that's to do with the anniversary or something she said happened at City Hall. Maybe you know about that; I guess you would've been there. At any rate, everything's fine here, and we're well accustomed to dealing with these anniversaries, Phil, and it was real good of you to call. Thanks for thinking of us."

"Sure thing, Gerald. We'll get together soon for a drink, OK?"

"Yeah, sure, that's fine. Have a good night," Gerald said, hanging up.

He went directly to the cookie tin and forgot all about the show on television. Instead, he stood in the kitchen, leaned against the counter, and ate one cookie after another, crunching and munching his frustrations away.

Phil irritated him, always had. When Mary Ellen agreed to marry him, he knew in his heart she wasn't over Phil. And for years after, he suspected Mary Ellen and Phil still sneaked around behind his back. He glanced at the picture of Savanna on the refrigerator, as he often did when Mary Ellen was out, and looked deeply in her eyes. Did she even look like him? Or did she look more like Phil Gravy?

And he was annoyed that Phil would even call to check on Mary Ellen. Didn't Phil know that Mary Ellen had a husband to look after her? He, Gerald, did not need any help keeping an eye out for his wife and noticing when she was doing poorly. That was his job, not Phil's job. How dare that man call every year, acting as though he was integral to the "take care of Mary Ellen's welfare" team? He was not part of it, no way.

And he was annoyed that Phil suggested they go out for drinks.

It was Phil's standard closing, something he said at the end of every conversation Gerald had with the man, and they both knew well that they'd been agreeing to have that drink for almost three decades. Had they had a drink together? No. Would they have that drink together? Nope. Why did the man insist on acting as though they were good buddies when they both knew the only thing they had in common was Mary Ellen?

Last, he was annoyed with Mary Ellen. It took him several cookies to work off that frustration, and still, he had a difficult time shaking it and letting it go. Everyone in the world, at some point or another, loses someone he or she loves. It's part of life. Mary Ellen, however, would never let the loss of her mother go, though it happened eons ago. She lived in the past, and he could not find a way to help her overcome the loss of her mother and move on.

Mostly, he felt that she could let it go if she knew the truth about whether her mother was murdered, or she committed suicide. But the case was cold now, and they likely would never know the answer. Still, every year, he called Mark, the Police Chief, to see if there were any new leads on the case, hoping against hope that one day, some revelation would help Mary Ellen move on.

The Police Chief was of little help, though. Over the years, he had moved on, and now, Gerald's calls were an annoyance. Although it seemed a suicide, Mary Ellen adamantly refused to believe her mother would take her life.

Living was someone who keeps one foot in the past is difficult work. For example, reminders of the past filled their home. In the dining room, hung a portrait of Mary Ellen's mom, larger than any other picture in their home of anyone, living or dead. Once, Gerald suggested moving the picture to Mary Ellen's office, thinking, instead, to hang a nice family picture on the dining room wall. She acted as though Gerald suggested burning babies or using the family crucifix for firewood or anything equally sacrilegious.

"I want her close, Gerald," she said. "I don't want her to miss a thing that goes on in our lives."

As delicately as possible, he tried to hedge up to explaining to her that she was already missing everything, given that she had been dead for forty years, but Mary Ellen would have nothing of it.

"I know she watches over us; I know she does. She sees everything as though she never left. And you want to stick her back in an office where she can't hear our lives and smile down on us? What are you—some kind of monster?"

There was no winning that one, and Gerald backed off quickly once he saw the flames leap in her eyes. "OK, OK, I'm sorry; I didn't realize having her close meant so much to you. I get it now; she can stay."

But inside, as was often the case after such arguments, Gerald felt pushed aside. Their home—his and Mary Ellen's—would always have a reminder in it of the woman who shadowed their lives with the circumstances of her mysterious death. The worst part was, Gerald never met the woman. He moved to Cut Bank years after her death, fresh out of a two-year college where he studied how to be an administrative assistant, and Cut Bank ISD gave him a great job opportunity. By the time he moved to Cut Bank from Florida, Mary Ellen's mom was dead and gone, and she was coming out of a breakup with Phil Gravy.

Everyone always warns you about rebound dating, and he knew from the start that he was Mary Ellen's rebound after ending things with Phil, but he didn't mind. Girls weren't that interested in him because he was quiet in school and a little on the chubby side his whole life. When Mary Ellen struck a conversation with him in the line at the post office, he worried he would be sick all over her with the nervousness churning in his belly, but they'd talked, anyway. She was so delightful, so sweet, and charming, and her smile disarmed him.

The best part was she seemed interested in him from the beginning, as if she enjoyed talking to him. She had so many questions about Florida—whether there were sinkholes and whether people really disappeared in the Everglades. When it was her turn to step up to the postal counter, he gathered his nerve to slip his phone number to her, and she accepted it with a smile.

They dated for a year, getting together on weekends for a movie or dinner. He didn't see her much during the week during that time. She said she had busy workdays as a social worker and needed her rest, and he thought nothing of it. The work she did was important, and he wanted to be supportive.

When he proposed to her at Christmas, she accepted, but she delayed. It wasn't quite the romantic proposal he always envisioned, and she took the ring he offered from down on one knee (his knees complained about that maneuver for weeks after) and told him she would get back to him. And she did—three days later. She called him and said that she accepted his proposal, and that was that.

They had a spring wedding, and he was the happiest man on earth looking at this beautiful, energetic, important woman walking down the aisle to take his hand. He never felt more proud or more legitimate in the crazy world that seemed to have an appetite for swallowing up chubby, insignificant, quiet types. Mary Ellen oozed with importance, and he felt important under her umbrella.

Gerald looked again at the picture of Savanna. They never really bonded—he and his daughter. And their son—well, no one knew where he was these days. She had that cleft in her chin he became obsessed with over the years. Whose genes contributed such a feature? Mary Ellen didn't have a cleft, nor did he. But Phil Gravy did.

He often wondered whether Mary Ellen got over Phil. There were little things, things only a doting husband noticed, that made him wonder, such as her obsession with her mother's death and how she would get flustered and anxious at times. When he tried to talk her out of calling Mark and demanding the case be reopened, she hastily grabbed her keys and left the house. Where did she go on those nights she stayed out until dawn? To Phil?

And the Town Council meetings she insisted on inserting

herself into—why did they continue to be so important to her? Was it because Phil was there?

Then, she disappeared for a week, a year or so after they married. He was debilitated with worry. She left him a note, and she was gone, saying he shouldn't worry about her. How could he not? She was his little bird, his dove, his moon and stars! But she returned a week later as if nothing happened, saying she just needed to get away. Shortly after, she quit her job as a social worker and said she needed a change.

She opened a realty office, instead, and he was proud of her. He hoped her new venture would make her happier, and it seemed to. Suddenly, she was interested in sex again, after a long hiatus of intimacy. She wanted to have sex every night for several weeks after returning home from her week away. Then, one day, she told him she was pregnant, and he wasn't surprised. What surprised him was that as soon as she said she was pregnant, she lapsed quickly back into not wanting to sleep in the same room with him.

Things such as that make a husband wonder. But his mother always said marriage is a long road of forgiveness and letting go of doubt; we choose "happily ever after" each day of our lives, and it doesn't land on us like some fairy-tale ending.

He was committed to Mary Ellen, despite his doubts. He worked hard to let go of his suspicions about Savanna's paternity. He was Gerald—a kind, stoic, devoted husband who knew deep inside that no matter what Mary Ellen did, he would always be committed to her. Why? Because she chose him, and if he lost her, likely, no one else would.

CHAPTER 9

Gerald? It's Dana.
I think you need to pick up Mary Ellen.

—Dana

T
hings weren't right, and Mary Ellen was agitated. She felt as though people watched her everywhere she went. The lesbians at the coffee shop. The man at the grocery store who wanted to kidnap her and make her wear a burka. Even Gerald. Her own husband wouldn't stop staring at her. Couldn't she have a third drink in the peace and quiet of her office without her husband staring? God knows whiskey has fewer calories, anyway, than all the cookies and beers he always stuffed his face with, right?

She pulled up at a traffic light and stopped dutifully, well before the white line, like a model citizen. The guy in the car next to her was, she thought, also staring. When she looked at him, she was certain he turned his head away at the last second. She noticed he was Hispanic and wondered how many were in Cut Bank these days.

"What is wrong with these people? Does everyone in this town has a staring problem?" she asked aloud, banging her hands on the steering wheel for emphasis.

It was a typical workday, and she believed it would be busy.

A text from Dana, her assistant, earlier that morning sounded as though she would be walking into a mess when she got to work. "Big news; I'll fill you in when you get here," Dana's text said. A few minutes later, a second text came from Dana. "Take your time, relax, and enjoy the morning."

Pulling into her parking spot outside her realty office, Mary Ellen took several deep breaths before walking inside. *Maybe I just need to talk to Dr. Spence. Maybe it's time for new meds. Maybe no one is staring at me. Maybe it's all my imagination. Maybe my paranoia is creeping back. Maybe I should call him today. Maybe he won't want to talk to me. Maybe I should go to his office, instead. If I did, would he stare at me, too, like everyone else?*

Inside the office, Mary Ellen knew something was awry immediately. Dana had brewed a fresh pot of coffee, and next to Mary Ellen's mug, already laid out with creamer and two sugar packets, was a tray of chocolate éclairs.

"I brought in your favorite," Dana said cheerily.

"Why?"

"Oh, well, I just know you've been working hard, and I thought perhaps a special surprise might brighten things for you; that's all."

"I don't believe you," Mary Ellen replied, scowling.

"No, really! I just want you to be happy and enjoy your work," Dana replied, not convincingly.

"Spill."

"Spill what?"

"Spill whatever news you have to share, which I already know won't be good. I also know chocolate éclairs won't change it."

Dana sighed. She backed up from Mary Ellen and leaned against the front desk, bracing herself on either side with two hands clinched tight against the wood.

"Why do you act like you're on a ship that's about to sail through a storm? Why are you bracing yourself that way?" Mary Ellen demanded.

Dana hung her head and looked at the floor, but kept her hands clenched. "You're not going to like this."

"I'll be the judge of that. Out with it."

"Tim Hannon called this morning. You know, with Agro-Northwest."

"Yes, yes, I know who Tim Hannon is. We're inches away from negotiating the sale of a hefty chunk of land for him north of town. It's a huge contract."

"Yes," said Dana. "That's what he was calling about."

"Is he backing out of selling the property?"

"No, he just said he was going to list it with a new agent."

"A new agent? But why?" Mary Ellen was livid. She worked tirelessly to peddle a several-thousand-acre plot and list it nationwide, knowing that when it sold, her commission would pay her personal and corporate bills for the rest of the year.

Dana handed Mary Ellen a piece of paper. "This is the contract termination letter he sent as follow-up to the phone call. I think it explains it pretty well."

Mary Ellen ripped the page from Dana's hand, and her eyes hungrily scanned the page for answers. "Difference in philosophy . . . Corporate reputation . . . Need for congruency in sales style . . . What is this? It's a bunch of bullshit! Get Tim on the phone immediately! And you're wrong! This does not explain things very well at all! Get that man on the phone; I want answers," she shrieked, shaking the letter in the general direction of Dana's head.

Dana dutifully dialed the number, and after a few moments, Tim's voice was heard on the speaker in the office.

"Tim! I heard some distressing news this morning!" Mary Ellen crooned. Dana was always impressed by how quickly Mary Ellen could change from shrieking madwoman to soft-spoken professional in seconds. "Tell me what's wrong, Tim. Let's talk about this. I'm sure we can work it out. Your letter just doesn't quite seem to explain why . . ."

"Mary Ellen, I'm going to put it to you straight," Tim said. "We're both busy people, so let me just lay it out for you."

"Yes, of course! Please do!" Mary Ellen replied sunnily. Perhaps she could still salvage the relationship with her biggest client in twenty years of realty.

"I was served with three civil lawsuits this morning. They are sitting on my desk now, staring at me. Each of the three cites discrimination against potential partners of Agro-Northwest. This is your doing."

"My doing? I don't see how . . ."

"When you represent Agro-Northwest in negotiating sales of corporately held property, and you decline potential buyers based on their sexual orientation, their skin color, and their religion, it is called discrimination."

"Oh, that! Well, I just wanted to do what I could to get you a decent buyer, someone with cash, someone who wouldn't stiff you at the signing table and be unable to come through with the asking price! Everyone knows lesbians, minorities, and Muslims don't have any money!" It all seemed perfectly reasonable to Mary Ellen, and she couldn't understand what she did to set Tim off this way.

There was a long sigh on the phone. "This will be my last statement, Mary Ellen, and then, I am hanging up the phone without hearing your reply. We won't speak again. Ever. If you try to call me, I will not answer. If anyone from your office calls me, I will not answer. You see, this morning, as we speak, my PR department is scrambling, trying to do damage control against these allegations. The biggest piece of our strategy is to be able to say, truthfully, that Agro-Northwest has severed all ties with you as our realtor. I am doing that now.

"On a personal note, you are a very nice person and very good at your job, but take some advice. This is the twenty-first century, and we live in America. People are allowed to be whatever color they want, worship as they choose, and fuck whomever they please. You can't do business this way, Mary Ellen. Goodbye."

The line went dead. In a rage, Mary Ellen stormed to the tray of éclairs and began to throw them at Dana, one by one. Then, she curled up on the floor and started crying.

Dana walked calmly to the phone and dialed. "Gerald? It's Dana. I think you need to pick up Mary Ellen."

Hours later, after sleeping off a sedative Dr. Spence provided, Mary Ellen felt like her old self again—calm, reposed, determined, and in a strategic frame of mind. No calamity could resist being averted by a sedative and a solid strategy session. Every problem could be solved, and a perfect solution existed for every problem.

She sat at her computer in her office listening to the sounds of Gerald sleeping in the next room and sipping on a cup of chamomile tea he brought her before going to bed. He said he was worried about her, but he wasn't worried enough to stay up past his 9:15 p.m. bedtime, which he adhered to religiously. *The man's snoring sounds like a freight train*, she thought crossly. She slipped in some earplugs and got down to business. Snoring wasn't going to derail her, and she was determined to stay calm and productive.

Agro-Northwest was the parent organization backing up myriad smaller corporations who, together, had the largest corporate landholding in the northwest region. They bought up acreage as if it were going out of style, kept what could benefit the grain-producing arm of their operations, and sold the rest as needed when municipalities wanted to expand or developers wanted to invest in a new shopping strip or condos.

In recent years, they were even more aggressive in their land buying to keep up with the newly popular need for hops and marijuana. What they didn't use themselves, they sold. They held on to their land until they could get a profitable sale price out of it, and they were large enough to exact whatever profit they thought appropriate.

Becoming the realty representative for the Cut Bank area of the state and surrounding counties was a windfall for Mary Ellen, regardless of whether she listed or sold any properties,

Agro-Northwest kept her services on retainer and paid her nicely to be available to them, as needed. She would have to scramble to make up the lost revenue.

A mild sedative still coursing through her veins, she didn't feel daunted in the slightest by the sheer size of taking on a campaign against Agro-Northwest. Every company has an Achilles heel. There's vulnerability just waiting to be exploited in every organization, and she would find it, expose it, and wield it like a sword to create trouble for Tim Hannon. He deserved it.

Mary Ellen opened her web browser and began to search for Agro-Northwest's pressure point. Minutes turned into hours, and she stifled a yawn but kept on clicking through web pages, news briefs, and any site she could find. She was making progress.

She debated between going to the press with an anonymous tip that Tim Hannon had a weakness for child pornography and exposing their head corporate lawyer as an alcoholic with a drug problem, based on some suggestive social media photos she found on the woman's Facebook page. Then, a banner flashed across her screen. Not wanting to miss a single breaking news story, she had her browser settings configured to alert her when the AP picked up a story in her area, and it just had.

"Cut Bank Town Council member disbarred," it said.

All thoughts of Agro-Northwest dissipated as she clicked the link. Her eyes greedily devoured the news brief that opened in a new screen. Her teacup dropped from her hand distractedly, splattering its contents all over her keyboard.

"Dammit!" she exclaimed, rushing to the bathroom for a towel.

With the keyboard dried, she settled into her chair again and tried to think. Something about this story bothered her, and she closed her eyes to grasp at the fleeting thoughts in search of the one that resonated with her. The news brief was clearly about Phil Gravy, though it didn't mention his name, as no other lawyers sat on Cut Bank's Council. But Mary Ellen was puzzled. The news brief stated that investigations into possible bank fraud were ongoing and that this person's legal practice was already closed for months. Months? Why was Mary Ellen just now hearing about it, and why wasn't Phil summarily dismissed from the Council because of such an investigation? It made no sense.

The more she thought about it, the angrier she became. To think that someone would steal from a bank in one town and practice law like an upright citizen and sit on town council in another was unthinkable. Cut Bank deserved better. The hardworking, taxpaying citizens of Cut Bank deserved more from their Council. Hell, it's the reason she tried to be elected to Town Council herself! She knew what people needed and wanted in an elected official, and she was prepared to be the strong-armed voice of the little people, if elected. The town seemed to think she would do a great job.

At least, each of the three times she ran for council and the one time she ran for mayor, everyone she met around town said they voted for her. But somehow, she never was elected and lost elections one right after the other by a landslide. But here was Phil Gravy, crooked lawyer extraordinaire, elected to council despite his ethical and moral shortcomings. She could hardly wait to smear the Mayor for not doing something about this months ago, when Phil began to be investigated for bank fraud.

She logged into Facebook and began to draft a status update to her followers. "Mayor Travis? We know what you've done. How could you think that our town would benefit from a bank-robbing crook?"

She imagined the Mayor's face when he realized that the whole town knew before he did that a criminal was advising the Council, and then she stopped herself from posting her draft.

Something wasn't right. How could the Mayor not know? He was much better connected with the happenings in the surrounding towns than she was. Surely, he would have heard about Phil's troubles months ago when the investigation started. Mayors talked to one another, didn't they?

Then, it hit her. He already knows, and he did nothing about it. He chose to keep Phil on the Council. But why?

In that moment, she did something she never had done. She deleted her Facebook post, in essence, walking away from a perfect opportunity to make the Mayor look bad in front of all her followers. There was more to this story; she was sure. She needed more facts; she needed more information; she needed to understand why the Mayor sat on this allegation all this time and didn't dismiss Phil from Council. There was a bigger story here. Postponing a chance to dig in on the Mayor tonight for the bigger, juicier, more shocking story later, would be worth it.

She shut down her computer and picked up her phone. Noticing the time—2:30 a.m.—she thought it inappropriate to make any calls, so opted instead for a text message.

"Hi, Phil, hope all is well. Do you have time for lunch tomorrow?"

CHAPTER 10

Look what she's done to herself, look how weak she was, look how she gave up and couldn't handle all of us anymore, look how she swings from the rope, and look how dead her eyes are. Poor Mary Ellen. Poor, poor Mary Ellen.

—Brandon's Psyche

Brandon was disappointed to realize that the cycle of nightmares was beginning again. It happened every year around this time. *At least I work in a coffee shop,* he thought. *Plenty of caffeine available to get me through these long days that follow long nights.*

He wondered whether everyone in Cut Bank was also having nightmares, as the coffee shop was unusually busy all morning. Everyone seemed irritable, sleep-deprived, and cranky. Usually, Brandon adored his customers and the daily banter they exchanged. Some of his regulars were as close to his heart as any of the handful of people in town he considered friends. It was endearing to observe their life in five-minute, daily snippets of light chatter while they waited for their usual order to be ready, most of which he knew by heart.

Jeremiah, who worked at the logging plant, liked a triple espresso with one sugar, and he was thinking of proposing to Lila, his girlfriend for three years. Simone was the baker for the French café across the street. Though she had coffee in her shop, she chose to come to Brandon because she knew he had a soft spot for day-old baguettes, which she always brought one for him each morning. What Simone didn't know was that Brandon's baguette never made it home because another of his usual customers, Everett, was going through tough times and struggling to keep his family fed. He always ordered a $0.49 cent refill for his battered, aluminum coffee mug between his two jobs, and Brandon made sure Simone was safely tucked back into the French café before slipping the loaf to Everett across the counter. His kids loved it, he always said, because it made great peanut butter and jelly sandwiches, which is sometimes all they could afford for lunch and dinner.

But that day, after a restless night, Brandon struggled to be cheerful, and that his regular customers were grouchy made his job as a happy barista especially difficult. Jeremiah couldn't reach his girlfriend the evening before and wondered whether she was cheating on him. Simone grumbled about her yeast not rising and apologized profusely for giving him three baguettes instead of one to make up for the fact that they weren't her best batch and seemed rather flat and lifeless to her. Even Everett looked especially tired that day, though receiving three baguettes seemed to cheer him substantially.

Nearing lunchtime, the steady stream of customers finally abated, leaving Brandon a few long overdue moments to tidy the front of the shop. He began by straightening the chairs, picking up stray napkins from the floor, and refilling the self-serve station with fresh carafes of cream and packets of sugar. As he stood at the bay window looking out at Cut Bank's Main Street, he admired the way the sun shone, especially because the days of that week were especially overcast and cloudy. It was nice to see the sun again, finally, and it invigorated him. He stood in front of the window, closed his eyes, and let the sunshine soak into his face.

Just a few more hours, then perhaps a nap, he thought, yawning.

When he opened his eyes again, he noticed the first moments of what turned out to be an unusual scenario unfolding before his eyes. The first thing he noticed was Mary Ellen, pacing in front of Simone's café. She looked agitated, which wasn't anything new, and kept checking her watch. Brandon wondered whom she was waiting for and assumed she was meeting someone for lunch.

After growing even more restless, Mary Ellen entered Simone's café, and seconds later, Brandon saw her seated at a table, alone, in front of the café's Main Street-facing window, directly in Brandon's line of sight. He wondered whom she was meeting and felt sorry for them already, whoever they were. Clearly, she was pent up and ready to explode, and he wouldn't wish that on his worst enemy.

With no customers in the shop, Brandon continued to stand at the window, watching. The lunch crowd started to pick up, and several people, most of whom Brandon didn't know and a few he did, entered the café. But the seat next to Mary Ellen remained empty. She seemed to study the menu between glances at her watch. He thought it telling and a good thing for Cut Bank that Mary Ellen still wore a wristwatch. (She was old school and traditional, and he knew the watch belonged to her mother.)

If she had a smartphone, which most people these days consulted for the time in lieu of a watch, he wondered how much Mary Ellen would plague the town of Cut Bank with moment-to-moment social media updates on everything from litter in the street to where she spotted the Mayor and what he had for lunch. As it was, she saved her updates for her time in the evening at home, at her desk, he assumed, which kept Cut Bank's social media updates to a blessed minimum.

A man took the seat next to Mary Ellen then, and Brandon recognized him immediately—Phil Gravy. He must have come in the back because Brandon didn't see him enter the café from the main entrance off the street. Mary Ellen didn't rise to meet him; she simply stared at him and then glanced down once more at her watch as if to mentally note how egregious Phil's tardiness was.

Why is Phil lunching with Mary Ellen? I didn't realize they were even close these days, Brandon wondered.

The phone rang then, and Brandon scooted back to the coffee bar to answer it. He still waited to hear what the City Council decided about his rezoning request, and whenever the phone rang, he hoped it was City Hall. It wasn't.

He spent a few moments wiping the espresso machine and putting ingredients away before his curiosity got the best of him again, and once more, he resumed his post at the window. In the short time he was away, Mary Ellen and Phil ordered, and they were now being served. Salads, it looked like. Simone's café made the best salads—fresh mixed greens, tossed in balsamic vinegar and olive oil, topped with feta, cucumber, red onion, pecans, and the house-made croutons from Simone's baguettes. His mouth started to water and he began to think about his lunch.

Thoughts of what to do about the grumbling in his stomach distracted him only briefly because something caught his eye. The sun caught the glint of a fork, its metal reflecting and casting shards of light. Mary Ellen was waving her fork. Not a good sign.

She progressed to shaking her fists and talking quickly and expressively with her hands, and then, even from the 20 yards between Brandon and Mary Ellen, he could see she was flushed and angry. She stood then, pushed her chair back, and began to wave her hands wildly in Phil's direction. He, too, pushed back his chair and leaned close to her face, shouting, before stomping away from the table.

Brandon felt sad that he wouldn't see Phil better as he exited the shop because Phil parked in the back. But wait, what was that? Phil walked out the front entrance, which Brandon thought odd because he didn't enter that way. He could no longer see Mary Ellen in the window and assumed she must have gone to the ladies' room. He could not help wondering what the disagreement was about.

Phil left Simone's café and walked angrily down the street, stopping at the hardware store owned by Kris, Mary Ellen's longtime friend, which was also odd to Brandon. Who leaves a lunch date angrily and goes next door to the hardware store? If he walked to the park, or came across the street to my shop for some tea to settle his nerves, or even went down to the end of the block to the bar for a quick tumbler of liquid peace, any of that would have made sense. But a hardware store? What? Did he suddenly remember he needs new light bulbs?

But odd or not, he went into Kris' hardware store. Brandon continued to watch as Mary Ellen got in her car and drove away, and Phil stayed in the hardware store. When he emerged, he carried a long coil of nylon rope in one hand and a roll of duct tape in the other. Then he was gone, out of Brandon's view, and the phone rang again.

Hours later, Brandon nursed a beer while lingering in the steam of the shower. He hoped the alcohol would make him drowsy enough to sleep dreamlessly that night, something he desperately needed. His afternoon was busy, and there was not much time to think more about what he witnessed, but now in the quiet of his home, he thought again about Phil and Mary Ellen.

Phil was known as a hothead, and Mary Ellen was known as the anxious, fly-off-the-handle type. For the life of him, he could not figure out how those two dated for as long as they did. At first, Brandon assumed Phil was a rebound for Mary Ellen, someone to take her mind off her mother's death and the ending of his and Mary Ellen's blossoming, though juvenile, relationship. But the longer they stayed together, the more he wondered how they survived without killing each other.

Of course, Mary Ellen was different back then. She was still high-strung, even back then, and had been for as long as Brandon knew her, but she had a softer side. She was kind, thoughtful, and went out of her way to help others. She was dedicated to her work—gut-wrenching, patient work with the foster program—and yet, she was full of grace and care for others. Now, in the decades after, Brandon watched from a distance as she hardened before his eyes, becoming bitter and quick to anger, eager to point out the flaws she saw in others, and not eager to apologize or even acknowledge her own.

Just be glad you weren't saddled with that broad, man. Good that you got out when you did, he counseled himself.

But it still bothered him, because it seemed a tragedy for such a once-beautiful girl to become a pill-popping, angry mess of a woman. Though he was uncertain how much of her current state had to do with the medications Dr. Spence had her on, her underlying psychiatric issues, or the death of her mom, clearly, Mary Ellen was on the fast train to Self-Destructville, and there wasn't much anyone could do about it.

That night, after sleeping soundly for several hours, Brandon was awakened by nightmares. They were different this time, though. He usually dreamed of Sue, Mary Ellen's mom, swinging from a rope in her closet with a note by her side that said, "I didn't do this to myself," which always woke him pondering what those cryptic words meant. Was it a subliminal indicator that he should suspect Sue didn't commit suicide, that perhaps she was murdered, or was it meant to incriminate Mary Ellen as the person who drove her to her final actions, and Sue believed Mary Ellen was the only one to blame?

That night, though, Sue didn't hang from the rope. In his dream, he walked up to Mary Ellen's home, and Gerald answered the door, his hands red and blistered as if he struggled with something or someone. "I wanted to check on Mary Ellen; I'm worried about her," Brandon said to Gerald in his dream. Gerald signaled Brandon to enter the house and head toward the master bedroom. When Brandon arrived, Mary Ellen was there, at the end of a rope, surrounded by Phil Gravy, the Mayor, and Sue.

"Look what she did to herself, look how weak she was, look how she gave up and couldn't handle all of us anymore, look how she swings from the rope, and look how dead her eyes are. Poor Mary Ellen. Poor, poor Mary Ellen," they all said in a haunting, unanimous voice.

He ran from the room then, eager to be out of the house and out in the light of day, but the Mayor called after him as he ran. "This is good for you, Brandon. It means there's no one in the way of your rezoning application getting approved now, no one at all."

Brandon woke in a cold sweat, his peaceful rest again disturbed for the third night in a row. He looked at the clock and noted the time—4:30 a.m. He knew he wouldn't go back to sleep, and so he dressed for work.

As he left for work, he committed to call Mary Ellen in the next day or two. As much as she was something of a joke to him and someone he felt sorry for, his dream reawakened a care for her he could not deny. She needed friends now, perhaps more than ever, and as one of her oldest friends, he felt responsible to step up and be there for her as best he could.

Her purposefully sabotaging his goals of opening his brewery mattered little. When a friend needs you, you go to your friend and put your arm around her. And in the case of a friend such as Mary Ellen, you hoped and prayed she wouldn't bite. But that, as they say, is simply the nature of the beast, which seemed especially appropriate in Mary Ellen's case.

CHAPTER 11

As he spoke, the Mayor mentally framed the schmooze job he'd have to pull to get an unsolicited, unscheduled phone session with the busy governor. The good news was, he was good at schmooze, especially where female assistants were concerned.

—Mayor Roy Travis

Mayor Roy Travis yawned. He looked at the pile of paperwork on his desk, the jar full of his favorite black ink, fountain pens in mahogany casings, which the taxpayers didn't know he bought, among other things, and rang the receptionist.

"Another cappuccino, Jill."

He slept well the night before; poor sleep wasn't the reason for his yawns. He golfed well the afternoon before; lack of recreation, sun, and exercise weren't responsible, either. It was boredom, of that he was sure.

Being Mayor of Cut Bank was about the easiest job a person could have. It ranked right up there, he thought, with being a kindergarten teacher (how difficult is it to sit a bunch of kids at desks and watch them color all goddam day?), being a secretary (all you have to do is bring the boss a cappuccino when he asks for it), and being his wife (all she does is lie around and watch television and fold some socks every now and then, right?).

Still, boring or not, he already knew there was no job he'd rather have. Being mayor means you are at the top of the heap. You call the shots. You are the master of your ship, and anyone who says otherwise can go to hell, a fact the Mayor had no problem reminding dissenters.

But it was boring. Take today, for example. The Mayor had to review the transcripts from the last Council meeting and sign off on them, attesting to their accuracy (hence the stack of papers in front of him). He had to review the budget and their last quarter's expenditures compared with the budget (easy work because if the two didn't match, Jill would be instructed to massage a few digits here and there, immediately, even if she had to work late). Then, he had a meet-and-greet at the local library with a philanthropist gifting Cut Bank with a large collection of children's books (why kids would go to the library and check out books these days when iPads had a Kindle app was beyond him). An easy, easy day, and so, so typical.

Lately, Mayor Travis had begun to think there might be more for him out there in the big world of politics. He mastered the stage that is in Cut Bank, and perhaps, it was time for a bigger scene. When you are a puppet master not only adept at pulling the strings, but who also designed the strings you pull, politics cease to be a fun game and begin to rank up there with family outings to the zoo and watching your kids play high school sports—on the boring scale. Is there anything droller than being the Mayor of a town such as Cut Bank where nothing exciting ever happens, and everyone is well trained not to cross you?

It was easy work, an easy paycheck, and occasionally, it gave him insight into profitable investment opportunities, but outside that, it was boring. Even worse than boredom was the fact that he didn't get nearly enough press time.

The Mayor pulled a handheld mirror from his desk drawer—its only contents—and gazed at himself. He was still in great shape. Botox kept him from wrinkling, golf kept him tan and fit, top-shelf whiskey kept him relaxed, and the girls over at The Office (he always thought that was a clever name for a whorehouse) kept him fit and virile. Yes, he was a fine, fine specimen of a man, and the news outlets didn't get him on camera or in the papers nearly as often as they should.

It's a crime to hide a successful, handsome politician like me in a little, sleepy town like Cut Bank, he thought, putting away his mirror and ringing Jill again.

"Uh, Jill? Don't know whether I specified this, but I wanted that cappuccino today, not tomorrow, and if you bring it next week, I'll can your ass."

He mentally noted to look up Jill's salary and have her draft an executive mayoral order to dock it 20 percent, for his signature. She might have kids and a family to support and, hell, she might even have an elderly parent or four she cared for, but all that meant to him was that she should have plenty of motivation to look lively and act as if she wanted to keep her job. And because the girls at The Office weren't as good-looking anymore, he might expand Jill's job duties soon. Maybe if she were compliant, he'd decide not to dock her salary.

Yes, it was time for a bigger stadium, something better suited to his skills, motivation, and good looks. Something bigger than Cut Bank, that was what he needed. Maybe the Governor's seat was next up, and from there, perhaps it would be time to throw his hat in the ring for the presidency. Yes sirree, Mayor Travis was going places.

He thought about the Governor, a wrinkly codger with the bad fortune of being named Jeff Jeffries, and wondered how long it would be until he was up for reelection. Seems like it is about time for a new governor, doesn't it? Yes, he recalled seeing something about a few candidates throwing their hat in the ring. Did he have time to organize a candidacy campaign? Well, sure he did! Candidates such as Mayor Roy Travis aren't really candidates, are they? They just swing the pendulum in their direction, pay some people to make it look like they're campaigning and to line up the right hands to shake and palms to grease, and his victory was assured!

There was only one problem—Jeff Jeffries. What if he sought reelection as opposed to retiring from office at the end of his term? The mayor needed to have that bit of information for planning purposes.

"Jill? Jill? *Jill!* Get the Governor on the phone, and do it faster than you prepared my cappuccino, which I still don't have!"

"Sir? The new order for cappuccino mix is on your desk, waiting for your signature on the PO. It's been there for more than a week. As of now, we're out of cappuccino," Jill said over the phone, her voice dripping with equal parts fear and respect. Or maybe they were the same—she respected him because she feared him.

"Do you think that's the answer I want? Go down the street to that coffee place across from Sabine's, and get me a cappuccino! I'll sign the PO when I'm ready to and not a moment before! And before you go, get the Governor's office on the phone!"

"Yes, sir."

A half-second later, the phone in his office was connected to the Governor's direct line, and his assistant answered the phone cheerily.

"Good morning, Governor's office, Christine speaking. How may I help you today?"

"Good morning, Christine. This is Mayor Travis calling from Cut Bank. How are you today?"

As he spoke, the Mayor mentally framed the schmooze job he'd have to pull to get an unsolicited, unscheduled phone session with the busy Governor. The good news was he was good at schmooze, especially where female assistants were concerned.

"Just fine, Mayor. I'll connect you to Governor Jeffries now. Please hold a moment."

Her response was unexpected and efficient. Mayor Travis relaxed. This would be a fantastic phone call, and all because his name—his power, his prestige, and his awesomeness as a mayor—preceded him. Even the assistants knew they were expected to open the door for him. He pictured it—a small Post-It note at Christine's desk with his name on it, topping a short list of other mayors in the state, and the heading read, "Mayors who can call the Governor directly, no appointment needed."

"Governor Jeffries here, talk to me," came the voice of the Governor. It was a dichotomous mix of authority and weakness, like the voice of someone used to holding power and now weary of its weight.

"Jeff, so good to speak to you today. How are things in the driver's seat?" It was bold to refer to the Governor by his first name, but Mayor Travis was a bold man. Only bold men make bold strides.

"Most of my friends and close colleagues call me Jeff. You are welcome to call me Governor Jeffries," he said, his tone changing to disapproval.

Reeling and back-pedaling, Mayor Travis regrouped. "Of course, Governor. Noted. Now, how are things?"

He was relieved to hear the Governor's tone lighten again. "Oh, pretty good, pretty good. I have a hefty congressional session in play now, some big agenda items there. Recreational marijuana is the big topic now, as you know. Can't figure out for the life of me why these young people have enough time on their hands to smoke weed and then complain that there aren't enough jobs. Back in my day, you worked first and played later; it's not that way anymore. Kids today want to play and play some more and somehow expect a paycheck to drop out at the end of their bong into their lap . . ."

The ranting of an old man, Mayor Travis thought. *Yes, this state could do with someone more in touch, someone like me.*

"Well, take heart, Governor. It'll be someone else's problem soon, and you can spend your days relaxing with your grandchildren and golfing. What's the time on the ticker for your term? I've lost track . . ."

"I've got another two years," he said.

"Well, though I'm sure it feels like forever, it's good news for us. Can't imagine anyone else running this state; you've done such marvelous work. That said, you know what they say, 'All good things must come to an end.'"

"Yes, that's what they say, isn't it? Well, you can believe me when I say I'll definitely take an active interest in this state's future. Though everything's up to the voters in the end, I'll do my dandiest to put a good candidate in front of them, someone who will carry on what I've started in protecting the best interests and way of life of the citizens of this great state."

"I'm sure you will, Governor. In fact, it's interesting you mention your plans for an active role with elections just around the corner. Actually, it's why I called."

"Oh? What's on your mind, son?"

Carefully, carefully, don't blow this, Mayor Travis counseled himself.

"I've been talking to the wife and family, and all my fantastic supporters over here in Cut Bank and a few friends, and everyone seems to agree I'm at a point where I'm primed and ready to make a difference on a larger stage. You know; bring the good work I've done in Cut Bank to the state level. We run under budget consistently, thanks to an active City Council and

productive new business and revenue streams. It's not many cities—you'll agree—that can boast of being in a budget surplus, year after year. And there are my staffers, a happy lot . . ."

"I'm gonna stop you right there, son," the Governor cut in.

"Of course, of course. It's why I called—so we can have a nice back-and-forth conversation about my . . . Well, let's just be honest . . . I'm calling to talk about my gubernatorial chances, with your support, of course."

"That's your first mistake right there, son."

"Oh? How so?"

"You don't listen. A good governor must be a good listener, first. Else, how will you hear the needs and wants of the people you serve?"

"Oh, well, I think I'm a very good listener, actually." Mayor Travis was confused and starting to feel as though a train wreck was in his distant future.

"No, you don't. I said, first thing, I would support a candidate who would continue the work I've started, and that's where you stopped listening."

"I don't understand . . .," Mayor Travis said, an unusual meekness in his voice.

"Let me be crystal clear then before your ears flap shut again," the Governor said. "The people in this state love me. Why? Because I run a tight ship, am honest with the people I serve, and keep this state headed in the right direction—a positive, productive direction."

"I hear you. I hear you. I feel the same way about the leadership I've contributed in Cut Bank."

"Again, sorry, but I'll interrupt just for the sake of time. I'm glad you called today because I was actually planning to call you myself to arrange a visit to Cut Bank. You have created an eyesore of a PR mess down there in Cut Bank. It's all over social media, and national outlets are starting to cover it too. I've known for a long time now that I need to step in and do something about it. A disbarred lawyer on City Council? Usurping the voice of the people by disregarding petitions in zoning matters? Need I go on? No, I don't. If you want to see what I see, look at the social media pages of your town's public voice. It's a loud voice, and it's being heard."

Mayor Travis felt the floor dropped out from under him. He knew what the governor referred to—Mary Ellen and her social media campaign against him.

"Governor, I . . ."

"No, son, I don't have the time to argue with you. Best clean up your backyard before you start looking to move up to a bigger neighborhood. This state doesn't need you warming my chair and giving us a black eye. Get on it, son. Get that mess cleaned up or I'll do what I can to make sure your political career ends for good. A good day to you. I have another call coming in."

The line went dead, and Mayor Travis felt his mouth go dry.

"Where's that cappuccino and get Spence on the phone!" Mayor Travis yelled into the intercom.

"Roy? Where's the fire?" Dr. Spence asked, a moment later, sensing some urgency from an unknown source.

"The fire is right here in Cut Bank. Something must be done about Mary Ellen, once and for all."

"Meet you at the country club tonight. I'll get us set up. Don't worry, Roy. We'll get this under control. You're right; it's time." Dr. Spence had not had opportunity to share with the Mayor that Mary Ellen refused a new prescription for meds, and he worried what the repercussions would be if he couldn't keep her medicated and under their thumb.

Mayor Travis hung up the phone and pounded his fist on the desk, spilling his cappuccino on the desk. "Jill! Get me another one!"

CHAPTER 12

I don't need any doctors! I'm not sick! Just because you fools don't see what's going on here doesn't mean I'm the one with the head problems!

—Mary Ellen

"**G**erald! Gerald, can you get the door?" Mary Ellen screamed from her office. *Where is that man? I swear he infuriates me to no end some days. I'm here trying to work, trying to save our town from the likes of that crooked mayor, and he's watching some game show and being utterly unhelpful,* she thought. "The door, Gerald!"

Sighing, Mary Ellen got up and moved to answer the door and see who incessantly rang the doorbell. As she passed the living room, she saw Gerald napping in his chair and groaned loudly.

"This better be good," she muttered, yanking the front door open with a homicidal strength.

"Your mailbox is full, ma'am," the postal carrier informed her. "I had no space to leave today's mail, so thought I'd better hand-deliver it. Oh, and just wanted to thank you for that bit of news you passed along on Facebook, the one about how the Mayor plans to change the hours of the post office to include Sundays, so he could get packages delivered that day. We, all of us, appreciate the heads up."

Mary Ellen warmed to the man, despite the poor timing of his knock on her door. "I'm here to serve," she said and wished him a good day.

The rest of the day went downhill quickly. At the bottom of the hill, it nosedived into a ravine that opened into a dark, underground canyon. At the canyon bottom, her day found an opening that took her into the center of the earth, straight into the pit of hell—all because of the postal carrier's delivery.

"Geeeeerrrrrrraaaaalllllldddd!"

Napping or not, Gerald rushed to Mary Ellen's side. It was that kind of shriek. But Mary Ellen wasn't injured, and she didn't spontaneously combust, as her screams would lead you to think. She sat cross-legged on the floor, looking unharmed and uninjured. In her lap, she cradled a book.

"This. *This!*" She flung the book at him.

Gerald picked it up and instantly wished he hadn't been lazy and neglected a trip to the liquor store. He would need a stiff drink; he knew that.

How to Commit Suicide showed a picture on its cover of Gerald and Mary Ellen's daughter Savanna. It wasn't just any picture, though; it was a picture of Savanna locked in a passionate embrace with a woman, their lips hungrily sharing their desire for each other.

"She's a lesbian? Our daughter! Did you . . . Did you know about this, Gerald? Did you!" Mary Ellen screamed.

"Well, I suspected it, actually, but she's never come out to me about it," Gerald said. He moved to his wife's side, extending a hand and trying to comfort her. "If our daughter's a closet lesbian, don't you think there are worse things? I mean, at least she knows what makes her happy, right?"

"You know damn well how I feel about homosexuals, Gerald. Damn well! It will not be tolerated, not in this family! That's the devil's business, and I raised her better than that!"

Gerald sighed; he'd heard it all before. His wife wouldn't tolerate so many things.

"She's your daughter, honey. A mother's love is unconditional; remember? Besides, we don't even know whether she's a lesbian. Someone sent us this book, but it could be a bad joke, right? I mean, the title alone says it all. It's a gag! *How to Commit Suicide*? What does that even have to do with homosexuals or our daughter?"

"Don't you see? It's happening again! Mom got a book, just like this, just before she died. Only it had a picture of me on the front, kissing Brandon. And now, she's dead!"

"Let me get your meds, dear. You're headed for a fit; we both know it," Gerald said, trying to stay in control of the situation as he stormed from the room.

"I don't need any meds!" Mary Ellen retorted. She began to pace and rant. "I will not have a lesbian in this family! And who sent me that book, and where has it been all these years? I know I saw it before, just with a different cover. I thought Phil got rid of it! He told me he did! It was the only thing linking me to the scene of Mom's death, the only thing that made me look like a suspect! He told me he sacrificed his detective career stealing that book from the evidence room and getting rid of it! I thought it was gone!"

"Just hold tight, dearest. I'll bring you your pills, OK?" Gerald called from the other room.

"I don't need any of those damn pills!"

She was unraveling quickly, and it reminded him of the time she ransacked the entire house and broke her mother's china, which made her even angrier when she learned her hairdresser had an abortion. Little uncontrollable things in her world that were none of her business set her off.

As he rummaged through the medicine cabinet in the kitchen, he dialed Phil's number, but got no answer. He left a message. "Phil, it's Gerald. If you aren't busy, swing by today. She's in one of her fits. You might be able to help. If you could help, you know, to calm her,

I'd be forever grateful. I know you have a way with her, and I . . . I . . . well, I need your help."

Though he spoke quietly into the receiver, it wasn't enough to prevent Mary Ellen from overhearing.

"I don't need to see Phil Gravy, OK? I don't want to! I don't want to! Don't you dare invite that fraud over here! I don't need disbarred lawyers in my house, and I don't need lesbians, either! You keep that man away from me, you hear?"

"I'm going to call Dr. Spence; OK, honey?"

"I don't need any doctors! I'm not sick! Just because you fools don't see what's going on here doesn't mean I'm the one with the head problems!"

From the kitchen, she heard Gerald on the phone.

"Yes, something stronger this time, I think . . . And maybe something powdered? I just don't think she'll knowingly swallow anything this time . . . Very good . . . I'll slip it in her juice . . . Yes, thank you . . . I'll pick it up right now."

"Honey? I'm going out for a minute. Why don't you take a hot bath? I'll be back in a jiff," Gerald shouted, unaware that Mary Ellen hid just around the corner from the kitchen phone and heard every word. Gerald grabbed his keys, walked to the car, and headed for the liquor store and the pharmacy, in that order.

As he drove, he pulled out his cell phone and made another phone call. This time, it was to Savanna. She didn't pick up, so he left her a message. "Hi, Savanna; it's Dad. Something is upsetting your mother, so I just wanted to ask you to please not call for a few days until I can get her medicated and back under control. It's about you. She thinks you're a lesbian. And it's OK with me if you are, but she's not handling it well. Call me in a few days, and we'll talk it through. Love you, baby girl."

Mary Ellen did few things her husband recommended, but the idea of a hot bath seemed to be good, so for a change, she took his advice. In a steaming pool of bubbles, she considered the book she received and again wondered about its source. Images of the picture of Brandon and her on the cover of her mother's version of the mysterious book filled her mind, and for the millionth time, she wondered how anyone even snapped a picture of Brandon and her. They had dated so briefly; how did anyone even see them together, let alone snap a picture of her kissing him? It puzzled her for years.

After her bath, she threw the book in the trash and decided she wouldn't let it bother her. If Savanna were a lesbian, she would wait to pass judgment until she heard it from her daughter's lips.

The bath relaxed her enough that she was noncombative when Gerald returned home. She didn't argue when he poured her a glass of wine, and only afterward, as she slipped under the curtain of a deep sleep, did she even think to question whether he added Dr. Spence's medication to her Pinot Grigio.

But the book didn't disappear; it was in the mailbox the next day when she arrived home from work. She threw it away again. The next day, she found it tucked under her wiper blade as she got in the car in the grocery store parking lot. The day after that and for many days afterward, she found it in odd places—tucked between her front door and the screen, under the birdbath in the yard, tucked neatly under the phone on her desk at work.

The last day she saw the book, she found it in the strangest place of all. She went to the garage on a Monday morning to get in her car and drive to work. Her detached garage was always locked, as was her car. Mary Ellen believed in protecting your property from hoodlums and vandals. There, on the front seat of her locked car inside her locked garage, was the book.

In a fit of rage, she grabbed it from the seat and stomped out to the alley, intending to throw it in the dumpster. Her toss missed its mark and landed on the street, instead. She was running late and decided not to retrieve it and place it in the dumpster; rather, seeing it there on the road through the alley, she decided to leave it where it landed and hope the day's traffic ran over it and shredded it.

When she returned from work that day, she looked out in the

alley, and to her delight, the book was gone. She thought she'd never see it again. She also didn't stop thinking about it.

That she couldn't stop thinking about the book and the brazen image of two homosexuals kissing on the cover was why she didn't argue when Gerald handed her a glass of juice each evening. Chalky and bitter, she knew it was medicated, but the oblivion she needed as respite from thinking about the book was in that glass of juice, and she drank it dutifully.

Two weeks later, Gerald got the nerve to suggest Mary Ellen call Savanna. "You haven't spoken to her in a long, long time, dear. Don't you think it's time you call her? Oh, and maybe invite her for a girls' weekend? I'm going to be out of town early next week, and wouldn't it be nice to have some company?"

"No."

"She's your daughter, Mary Ellen . . ."

"No."

"Are you going to avoid her forever, on the off chance some hoax is true, and she might be a lesbian, which really is none of your business, anyway?"

"Yes."

Gerald sighed. He noted mentally to try calling Phil again the next day, though Phil was surprisingly unresponsive to his calls. He would try again. For once, he acquiesced that perhaps Phil was the only person who could talk some sense into his wife.

CHAPTER 13

May I speak to Detective Gravy, please? It's Casey from the neighborhood the death van came that night.

—Casey

"Hello?"

"Hi, Mary Ellen. It's Dr. Spence calling. I heard from Gerald you had some tough days of late, and I wanted to check with you. Everything going OK?"

"No, nothing's going OK. I'm a failure as a mother, and somehow, I managed to raise a lesbian daughter, and I have to take these new meds—obviously, you know that—so I'm not so upset all the time, and they're making me groggy-headed, and I can barely function," Mary Ellen said.

It was a Saturday morning, and Gerald was out of town for a work meeting. She wondered to what type of meetings school secretaries went. Did they have support groups for how to handle difficult principals, seminars on how to get chewing gum unstuck from the underside of the bleachers, or perhaps, continuing education on latest breakthroughs on recognizing the early signs a student isn't using a #2 pencil on a standardized test? The man was a colossal bore, but on his rare weekend away, she missed having someone with whom to chatter.

She answered the phone out of loneliness, and out of loneliness, she opened up to Dr. Spence. Usually, she didn't trust the man, never did.

"I'll tell you what, Mary Ellen. I'm here at the office today catching up on some paperwork, and I could squeeze in a session with you later this evening if you want to come by. Perhaps, if we can talk through some things bothering you, we'll both feel comfortable tapering some of the drugs you're on to help you regain quality of life. How does 6:00 p.m. sound?"

"Sure, Doc, I'll be there," she said.

"See you then," he said, clicking off the call.

The pills, the consults with Dr. Spence, the boring life with Gerald, her absent and, apparently, lesbian daughter, the whole disappointment of life wore on her. What was it all for, and would she ever feel happy and excited about anything again?

She doubted the impromptu session with Dr. Spence would do any good, but she didn't have anything else going on and figured it would be good to get out of the house. Maybe she'd even swing by Sabine's afterward for a salad or say hello to Brandon and have coffee. At least she knew she needed to try to do things she once enjoyed, but every day of the last few weeks felt as though she stared down a dark tunnel that bore an uncanny resemblance to a gun barrel.

After showering, Mary Ellen walked to the bedroom she shared with Gerald and opened the closet door to choose an outfit. Perhaps, it was the way the sun suddenly darted behind a cloud and darkened the room around her; perhaps, it was the medications she took, perhaps, it was the quiet of her house and the loneliness she felt. Whatever it was, nostalgia nearly swept her away, and for several moments, she relived every sensation of finding her mother hanging in that closet.

It was as if she were transported back in time to the moment when she found her swinging from the rope. Fear and sadness gripped her then, and an odd sense crept over her and enveloped her in shadow—was it a feeling of purpose, of knowing what she needed to do next, or a feeling of panic, that she needed to run immediately from some unseen threat? She could not have said which of the two it was, not with any certainty.

Her heart beat quickly, and she grasped the side of the closet door to steady herself. That's when she saw it. She leaned over and picked up the object from the floor, which had caught her eye. It was the book, and on its cover, was her daughter. This time, her lesbian lover sat beside her, her head on Savanna's shoulder, and a child sat on Savanna's lap, between the two women. The little boy wore a T-shirt with the words, "I love you, Grandma Mary!"

Mary Ellen never made it to her 6:00 p.m. session with Dr. Spence.

Was it right, or was it left? Why do they name the streets like this? Why can't they just put up an arrow that tells me the way to my house?

Casey stood at the corner of Elm and Ash, scratching her graying head and trying to recall which street, named after stately trees she had never seen, was the street on which she lived. Then, she remembered that when she felt confused this way and had this question, she was supposed to do something . . . but what was it?

She felt a tug and looked down at the leash she held, which she forgot she was holding, connected to the collar of the poodle she was walking, which she forgot about as well. The poodle, Beacon, tugged at her, and she noticed the letters embroidered on his collar—"Go home." Then, she remembered. She only needs to read those words to Beacon, and he would help her find her way home. Beacon knew Ash from Elm; Beacon would bring her home.

She lit a cigarette and followed Beacon through the fading light. It was nearly dark by then, and she did not want to get lost again, so she stayed close to her dog and clutched his leash tightly, as if her life depended on it. As she crossed the street, she saw a strange car, a dark sedan she saw long ago. She watched from the sidewalk outside her house as it circled the block again, more slowly this time. She lit another cigarette and, by the end of her third cigarette, she thought she was up to counting ten trips the car made around the block, but she couldn't remember if it might have been more than that. She lost track.

A memory came over her then, from long ago. She saw the dark sedan before and spoke to Detective Gravy about it. She wondered whether he might want to know that, forty years later, it was back in the neighborhood.

"Come, Beacon," she said, leading her dog into the house. "We'll call the detective."

The woman who answered the phone at the police station was very nice. Casey remembered that about her from the last time.

"May I speak to Detective Gravy, please? It's Casey from the neighborhood the death van came that night."

"I'm sorry, dear. Detective Gravy hasn't worked here in nearly forty years."

"Oh, OK," Casey said and hung up the phone. Forgetting she smoked at least three cigarettes not ten minutes ago, Casey picked up her pack of Camel Lights and went back outside.

Savanna parked her car outside her parents' home. It was months since she saw or even talked to her mom, though she and her dad spoke almost daily. Gerald said he would be out of town for the weekend, and it might be a good opportunity for Savanna to visit her mom under the guise of checking on her. "Perhaps, you could have a heart-to-heart talk with her, Vanny," he said, using his pet name for her.

Savanna was never close to her father, but recent events

improved their relationship drastically. It was the two of them now—Vanny and Dad—trying to help Mom get through a tumultuous time. During all the years she considered coming out of the closet, she always knew her mom would not support her through it. Her mom was a good reason to stay in the closet. Savanna didn't look forward to the day she told her mom about the lifestyle she chose, though she also never suspected her father would come to her side to support her.

"I don't especially care what you do in your bedroom, and I don't care if your partner is black, white, Asian, male, female, a firefighter or a banker. As long as you're happy and taken care of, I'll be happy too," he said.

"Mom will flip when I tell her, Dad," Savanna said on the phone the last time they spoke. "Any advice on how to break it to her? I mean, I feel like I can't move forward with my life until Mom knows. I'm tired of living a lie, and I'd like to bring someone home to meet the folks at some point, you know?"

"You're doing the right thing, Vanny. She's on meds now that help her stay steady. Go over, and check on her while I'm out of town, give her the meds, the powdered one, in her orange juice, and when she starts to get sleepy, tell her. That'll give her some time to mull over it in her sleep, and when she wakes, she'll have had time to process things. I think it'll work."

So, Savanna promised she would try. Now, sitting in the car outside her parents' house, she wondered whether it was still the best idea. Her heart pounded, and her palms grew sweaty. She stepped out of the car, gulping fresh air and hoping the cool night's chill would steady her. As she walked around the car to the sidewalk, she glimpsed her mother's neighbor. What was her name again? Candy? Cary? Casey? Something like that. *God, she's a strange one,* she thought.

Waving politely at the neighbor, she started to walk towards her parents' front porch, when Casey started screeching at her.

"Don't go! Don't go! The black sedan was here thirteen times, and then the death van will come! I tried to call for help, but the detective doesn't go to work anymore! The nice woman told me that on the phooooooooooooooone!" Her voice grew louder and louder, as if by yelling, she could tether Savanna to the car and keep her from encountering whatever Casey feared.

Savanna waved back. "Everything's fine; I'm just checking on my mom. Have a good evening!" *Nuttier than a pecan pie, that one is,* Savanna thought.

Casey watched her walk to the door and enter her neighbor's house, shaking her head "no, no, no," with each step Savanna took. Savanna entered the house and closed the door behind her.

Casey went inside her house, clutching her ears to keep from hearing what she knew would come next, but they heard it, anyway, though slightly muffled. It took less than a minute for Savanna to come running out of Mary Ellen's house, screaming for help. Casey watched from her front window, watched as Savanna made a phone call, watched as the patrol car pulled up, and later, watched as the death van came again.

Black sedan, circling, circling, circling, and then the screams, and then the death van. Casey tried to tell the detective, but he didn't want to hear it back then, and now, he doesn't work there anymore. But she lived on that street long enough to know. The young girl would probably be next; at least that's how the pattern worked. Casey knew all about the pattern.

It was Detective John Gray's first death investigation. When a young woman on Elm St. called in and said she found a body, dispatch radioed him at home where he was relaxing with his wife and new baby. The promotion to detective was more lucrative than he originally thought. Though he expected a raise and got one, the extra job perks that came with following the police chief's every instruction was unexpected—their mortgage was unexpectedly paid off, a new television was delivered, and the Chief, Mark Crew, hinted that something big was coming, and if John was helpful, how would his wife like a vacation in the Mediterranean?

Reluctantly, John dressed for work and kissed his wife goodbye. "I hope I won't be out too late," he said, "though it's my first stiff, so I don't know how that will go."

"Do what you have to do, John. We'll be here waiting for you," his wife said, kissing him sweetly.

Pulling up to the house on Elm St., he spent a moment talking to police already on scene.

"The premise is clear, Detective," one officer reported. "No sign of an intruder, and no one else in the house at the moment."

"Call the coroner then, Officer," John instructed. "I'll just take a quick look and then be back out to talk to the witness. It was the woman's daughter, right?"

"Right. Poor girl. To find your mother hanging from a rope in the closet . . . The girl is waiting in her car, trying to gather herself together before talking to you. The husband is on his way home from some work trip. Should be here in a few hours."

"Thank you; good report," John said and walked away, toward the house.

It didn't take but a minute to survey the scene and see what he was told to expect. He retrieved the evidence he was looking for, catalogued it quickly, and avoided the eyes of the woman hanging from the rope in the closet. He returned quickly to his patrol car and waited for the call he knew to expect. It came seconds later on his private cell phone, the one the Chief always used to reach him.

"Did you get the book? The one with the girls on the front?"

"Yes, sir, I've got it. Catalogued it right away, just as you said," John replied to the Chief.

"Good. Hang on to it. I won't let it get away this time."

John wasn't sure what the chief meant by "this time," but he knew better than to ask too many questions, especially not with a trip to the Mediterranean on the hook. He couldn't wait to take his wife shopping for their trip. She would look great in a black bikini on a sunny beach in Greece.

"You betcha, boss. I'll bring it to the station right away."

"Good man. Now, go finish the job."

"Yes, sir! Oh, wait— one more thing. There's a woman across the street yelling at the cops, saying she saw everything. Should I go talk to her?"

"Graying hair, dog, a cigarette, kinda crazy sounding?"

"Yep, that's the one."

"No, no need. I'll handle that on my end. She's crazy as a loon, anyway."

John hung up the call and emerged from the patrol car. He waved over the three cops who waited by the house for the coroner to arrive. "Gonna need your help, gentlemen," he said.

"You got it; what's up?"

"We need to make an arrest now, of the young woman in the car. Savanna."

"The daughter? But . . ." one officer started to protest. "On what grounds? Surely, you can't have determined this is murder versus suicide yet, not without the coroner and medical examiner here . . ."

"Chief's orders, boys. Take it up with the boss. Book her for suspicion of manslaughter. Bring her to the mental hospital; Dr. Spence will meet you there. I'll wait here for the coroner."

Casey and Beacon watched the girl go in the patrol car and drive away. The girl didn't want to go, Casey noticed. Then, the death van showed up, just as she knew it would, and the poor woman who was her neighbor and the daughter of her neighbor forty years ago took her last trip from her home. It made Casey sad. She wondered whether she should call the police station again. Maybe Detective

Gravy had come back to work now, and she could tell him all she saw.

She wavered about what to do and finished her cigarette, sending gray-blue smoke billowing into the cold night air, when she heard her phone ring inside.

"Hello? This is Casey and Beacon. Who is this?"

"Casey? Hi, it's your brother. Just wanted to call and check on you, see if you're still up for a visit with us in a month or so. I can buy your ticket if you want to come. How's Beacon?"

It was her brother's idea to get the dog, and she always wanted one, anyway. It was great having a brother who looked out for her. Casey liked visiting her brother; he was an important man.

"OK. Beacon and I can come. OK. OK. I have to go, Jeff. There's a thing going on across the street. I have to go watch. The death van came for my neighbor—my good neighbor, Mary Ellen."

"Mary Ellen? I know that name . . . What happened?"

"I have to go; I'll tell you tomorrow, OK, Jeff? Go on, go back to being the president, and I'll call you tomorrow."

"Uh, I'm the governor, not the president, but OK. Call me tomorrow."

Casey hoped she'd remember to call him the next day. Maybe he would know where to find Detective Gravy. He was an important man who knew many important things. She hoped she would remember to call, and she wished she knew how to make new reminder notes on Beacon's collar.

Instead of going back outside to watch, she went to her bookshelf and looked for any books she might have on how to embroider dog collars. She didn't find one, but that was OK because it was time for her frozen dinner and the news and that game they play where they spin the big wheel and yell, "Big money! Big money!" She liked that show.

PART 3: SAVANNA

CHAPTER 14

I would like to go to the Mediterranean too.

—*Savanna*

Sleepy. Groggy. Always so sleepy.

Savanna closed her eyes again and drifted back into sleep. It was all she did now. It was all she did for the past eight weeks.

Her thin hospital gown never felt warm enough, and she wasn't sure why she was even in the hospital. Was she sick? Reality and dreams floated together in a sea of oblivion, thicker than her mother's pea soup.

Mom. A man said she was dead. A man said that Mom killed herself because I kiss girls. He said if I sign these papers, I could go home. So, I sign them, and then Dad says the man took his money because I signed them, but all I did was try to get out of the hospital. Dad doesn't understand what the man promised me and how much I want to go home. Dad would have signed them too. The man reminded me of Thanksgiving dinner because his name was Gravy. I miss Thanksgiving.

Dad comes; sometimes, Dad comes. He looks sad when he's here, but then, I fall asleep and when I wake, he's gone.

A doctor comes. He tells me I have depression because my lifestyle led to my mom killing herself. I don't know whether I have depression because how can you be depressed while you're sleeping, and all I do is sleep. He tells me the medicine will make me better, so I take it.

The nicest man of all is the one with the pretty blue eyes. The doctor gives me a pill to wake, and the pretty man comes and stays with me. Then, he goes, and the doctor puts me back to sleep again. The pretty man holds my hand and asks me questions about what I remember. I don't remember anything, I tell him. That always makes him happy. He says he'll be gone for two weeks in the Mediterranean, but when he gets back, he'll visit me again. Gray. That's his name. I like that man. I would like to go to the Mediterranean too.

CHAPTER 15

I think I'll phone the governor again in the morning, to let him know I cleaned my room, and I'm ready for my reward.

—Mayor Roy Travis

"Gentlemen, to us!" Mayor Travis raised his glass, nodding appreciatively when Dr. Spence and Mark Crew followed suit. "To us!" the men echoed.

"I have to tell you . . . I feel like a man with a new lease on life," the Mayor said. He winked at the bartender to indicate his interest in a consenting adults "nightcap," as per their usual Tuesday evening plans, and to indicate he was ready for another round. "With Mary Ellen gone, I don't have to watch my back or worry about being dragged through the mud on social media for various and sundry preposterous reasons. I think I'll phone the Governor again in the morning to let him know I cleaned my room, and I'm ready for my reward."

"Just promise you won't forget your favorite psychiatrist when you hit the big time, Roy," chided Dr. Spence.

"And your favorite police chief," Mark added quickly. "After all, where would you be without us?"

"I'd be scrambling for air in bad PR stew, that's where I'd be, gentlemen. Now, enough celebrating. We have work to do."

Dr. Spence and Mark frowned. They were used to the Mayor's constant need to stay on top of business, but his transition from celebratory to productive seemed jaunty, even to them.

"And what's on our agenda tonight?" asked Dr. Spence.

"Philip Gravy's council seat," Mayor Travis whispered.

The Mayor might as well have stripped to his boxers in the middle of the country club; such was their surprise at his announcement.

"Well, now, this is news!" Mark said. "What happened to Gravy?"

"Nothing happened to him," the Mayor said. "At least, I don't think anything happened to him. He called me this morning, though, to say he was resigning his seat. Something about a rich old aunt dying and some inheritance money or some such thing. Maybe it was a rich old uncle; I don't know. Anyway, with as much trouble as he had with this business about being disbarred, he said he needed a break. The money came at just the right time, and I guess he's leaving Cut Bank. Going to Mexico or someplace."

"Any ideas on a replacement?" Dr. Spence asked.

"You mean a suitable replacement," Mark added. "Not just anyone will do."

"I know; you're right. It'll be tough. Our trusted circle is shrinking, gentlemen," the Mayor said. "I think it might be time for some new blood, some new recruits, someone who can give us an element of trustworthiness with the younger crowd. What about that new detective of yours, Mark? John Gray, is it?"

"Well, John Gray is young; you're right, Mayor. He's also in the Mediterranean at the moment and going through a little training, you might call it," said Mark.

"Training? In the Mediterranean? Sounds like a vacation to me," said Dr. Spence.

"It started out as one, yes. But before Gray left town there was a—how should I describe it?—a security breach, if you know what

I mean." Mayor Travis and Dr. Spence looked horrified, prompting Mark to quickly elaborate as much as he could. "He's been on watch detail with Dr. Spence's newest suicidal patient and has allowed himself to step out of character and develop a soft spot for the girl. Anyway, nothing major has happened, not that I know of, but he needs to be reminded of whom he works for. So, he's having a little training session, probably as we speak. When he returns, I guarantee you both, he'll be moldable—after he gets over his grief, that is."

"Sounds interesting," the Mayor said. "I'll leave you to it then; I trust you know what you're doing. How about you, Doctor? Any ideas on a suitable candidate for council?"

"Well, I thought about what you said about the younger crowd. There's a kid who works at the coffee shop—Brandon. You remember him, don't you? He wants to open a brewery downtown. Came to a council meeting once about a zoning request." Mayor Travis and Mark nodded. "He's not too young, but he thinks young, and he is in touch with the college crowd because of the coffee shop. Anyway, having him on board might be good representation for the African-American voters in Cut Bank and might help us look diverse and all that garbage."

Mayor Travis nodded slowly, thinking.

"Yes," he said finally. "I think you're on to something, Doctor. Why don't you stop by, talk to him, and see if you can get him on board? Let me know how it goes."

"You got it, Mayor. I'm on it."

Checking his watch, the Mayor stood to leave. "Now, if you'll excuse me, gentlemen, I have some other business to attend to before I go home to the wife and kids."

"Business? Is that what you call her these days?" Mark grinned, eyeing the bartender in the short black skirt and halter-top.

"Business, Tammy, whatever. Their names run together anymore. Good night, gentlemen."

CHAPTER 16

She could use the help, even if it came through a myste-rious midnight caller.

—Savanna

The covers lay twisted at her feet, remnants of another sleepless night. She wondered whether her phone would ring again at midnight, as it had a habit of doing every other night. Last night was quiet, so tonight must be the night.

The first time he called, she thought she was dreaming. Her phone never rang, and yet, it rang until she opened her groggy eyes from the depths of her pharmaceutically induced haze and realized it was her phone making all that racket. She answered it then, full of trepidation, wondering whether it might be John Gray calling from the Mediterranean. It wasn't.

However, it was a long-distance call, and it was a man. The caller identified himself only as a friend and asked whether she had a minute to listen. He said he was calling from far away, and he would do his best to keep tabs on her from a distance, if she'd let him.

That first night, she merely nodded at his suggestion that she begin to slyly slip her medications under her tongue without swallowing them and spit them in the toilet the minute the nurse left.

"They're keeping you drugged on purpose," the man said.

The second time he called, he made her promise she would take his advice.

The third time he called, she agreed.

Tonight, he would want to know how her ploy was going, and she was prepared with a full report and many questions. In the past 48 hours, she stopped taking all her meds and felt more alert, more so than she had felt in months.

The phone rang, and she picked up the receiver.

"Savanna? It's me. Your friend. How's it going over there?"

"I'll tell you after you answer some questions for me," she said defiantly.

"Ah, I see. I have my answer then. You're off the meds and thinking clearly again, and you have your feisty back once more. Good girl. Keep up the good work, Savanna. Remember, I'm here to help. I'll check back again soon. Sleep tight." The line went dead.

"Dammit!" Savanna swore under her breath, noisily hammering the phone receiver back on its base.

She spent the rest of the night trying to piece her life together and wondering why Melissa hadn't been to see her. She supposed her girlfriend didn't want to be associated with a psychiatric patient, but it would have been nice to at least hear it from her, instead of having to assume. She wondered, too, about John Gray and when he might be back from his vacation. Having slept the better part of three months, she suddenly felt wide-awake again, and the mere thought of sleeping anymore, ever, was just annoying.

So, she spent her days tricking the nurses out of her meds, systematically flushing them, and doing her best to appear groggy and pliable when they spoke to her. Her midnight caller said there was no point in arousing suspicion and that she had to be smart.

With her mental faculties now back to work, she began to piece things together, asking questions of her memory and trying to sort how she had ended up in a mental hospital in the first place. It was so unlike her; rather, it was so . . . Mary Ellen.

Two nights later, when he called again at midnight, she was ready for some answers.

"I need to know who you are," she said gently. "I appreciate your calls and your help; I just need to know who I can thank for the kindness of your care."

Her father always said you could kill more flies with honey than with vinegar, but her mother acted as though the opposite were true. Savanna was ready to try applying a heavy dose of honey now, in the hopes it would get her some answers.

There was a long pause on the other end of the phone, and then a heavy sigh.

"Please, at least for now, I need to stay anonymous. I can't help you—and believe me, you're going to need my help—if you know who I am. Suffice it to say, I am a friend of your family, and I'm simply trying to right some wrongs—some are my wrongs, some are the wrongs of others. Will you trust me?"

Savanna thought about the fact that she didn't have many friends to help her, and she had an uncanny deficit in visitors. She could use the help, even if it came through a mysterious midnight caller.

"For now, yes, I will trust you. What's next then?" she asked.

"I'm going to tell you a website link. You must write it down. Put it somewhere safe, and don't let anyone know you have it. Tomorrow, inform the nursing staff you're going home. If they say you can't, tell them you're leaving, or you'll call a lawyer to have them sued for medical malpractice, for holding you against your will and against medical necessity. Then, walk out. Your father will be there to pick you up at 2:00 p.m. and don't be late. When you get home, the first thing you must do is to access the web link I will give you. I'll be in touch."

"OK," Savanna said weakly. "I can do that. Give me the link when you're ready."

"Here it is . . . www.justiceformaryellen.org." The line went dead.

CHAPTER 17

You're looking for a seat warmer, an easygoing voice of agreement for whatever the Mayor wants; is that it?

—*Brandon*

Brandon was in no mood for customers and found it unfortunate his livelihood relied on them. Fragments of the most disturbing nightmares riddled his dreams, and he knew slapping on a fake grin and downing a triple espresso were his only options for getting through the day without killing anyone. He needed sleep, and he needed it badly. He wondered if it were time to speak with a doctor about a sleeping pill prescription; perhaps, Dr. Spence would write him one. Sue and Mary Ellen were six feet under and keeping the worms fed, so why did he continue to dream of them night after night?

The doorbell jingled, and he looked up to greet his first customer of the day.

"Speak of the devil," he said, seeing Dr. Spence enter.

"Well, I've been called many things, Brandon, but never the devil," the older man chuckled. "I'll have the usual, please."

Brandon ducked behind the espresso machine and began to work on the doctor's order—a double-shot vanilla latte with extra foam. While he worked, he thought of how he might broach the subject of some Ambien® with the doctor.

"Glad you're here this morning and alone," Dr. Spence said. "There's a matter of business—and one of some urgency—I hoped to speak to you about."

"Oh? And what's that?" Brandon asked.

"Well, I'll cut straight to it. City Council has an opening, and the Mayor wants you to agree to be nominated for it."

"Me? City Council? I . . . I'm flattered, really, but politics really aren't my thing," Brandon replied, flustered.

"I thought you might say that. Let me be candid, because I think you're precisely the man for the job, and we are prepared to make it worth your while," Dr. Spence said, edging closer to the counter and lowering his voice.

"Go ahead; I'm listening."

"The type of person we need on the Council is one who represents a minority here in Cut Bank and a person willing to go with the flow, not make any waves, and . . . well, you get my drift, don't you?"

"You're looking for a seat warmer, an easygoing voice of agreement for whatever the Mayor wants; is that it?" Brandon spent enough time watching Mary Ellen's vendetta against the Mayor play out, and he had a good idea how things worked in Council chambers.

"I like your direct approach, Brandon. A man who shoots straight is a man I would like to work with. But you make what I'm asking sound . . . oh, I don't know . . . scandalous, and it really isn't. It's just about encouraging Cut Bank's minority population to have some confidence in the Mayor's office—"

"So, you're asking me because I'm black; is that it?" Brandon interrupted, his eyes sparkling with edgy confusion.

"Oh, dear, I can see we got off on the wrong foot," Dr. Spence said, taking a step back and considering how to backpedal his way out of what turned into an adversarial conversation. "I am asking you, we are asking you, for a variety of reasons. There are reasons why you are the perfect fit, Brandon. Yes, you represent a cultural minority, but you are also a savvy business owner, and most important, Council is prepared to push through your rezoning request without delay and back your endeavor to open your bar."

"It's a brewery, not a bar," Brandon corrected.

"Yes, yes, of course. A brewery. So what do you say?"

Brandon thought about his dream of opening a brewery. *If I join Council, I get my brewery; if I don't, I might as well kiss that dream goodbye. They would stonewall me at every turn in retaliation. I know how these things work.*

"I need a prescription of something to help me sleep," Brandon said simply, randomly. "Is that something you can help me with?"

Dr. Spence smiled. "Absolutely, absolutely. Say no more of it; I'll call in the script directly."

Dr. Spence's phone rang then, and he pulled it out of his pocket to check the number. "I need to take this call; I'm sorry to cut this short. We will see you in the chamber tomorrow night then, for your confirmation?"

Reluctantly, Brandon nodded. Instead of feeling as though he just paved the way toward realizing his dream of owning Cut Bank's first brewery, the bile rising in his throat reminded him that what he agreed to was more in line with a bargain with the devil.

At least I'll get some sleep now and my brewery, and how difficult can it be to warm a chair and vote "yay" or "nay" as the Mayor directs? As soon as I get my brewery set up, I'll resign.

CHAPTER 18

Your mom was sick with many things—mostly grief and guilt.

—Gerald

"Talk to me," Dr. Spence said, walking out to his car, latte in hand.

"We couldn't stop her, Doctor. She's gone. She threatened a lawsuit and calmly walked out of the hospital. I tried to follow, but she had a ride waiting for her, and she was gone in the blink of an eye," the nurse said, exasperated.

"Wait a moment; whom are we talking about? The looney in room 2-C or the transvestite in 2-D?"

"Neither."

"Oh, God. Savanna?"

"Yes, sir."

There was a pause, and then, as cool as can be, Dr. Spence responded. "Don't bother coming to work tomorrow, Nelly. I told you all Savanna was a special case. You let me down. You're fired." He didn't wait for a reply before ending the call.

Two miles away, Savanna relaxed into the front seat of Gerald's car. It felt good to be free, and she could hardly believe how easy it was to escape the hospital, which felt like a prison.

"You OK, Vanny?" Gerald asked, merging on to the highway that led toward the home he shared with Mary Ellen.

"Yes, Daddy. I'm fine. I just have a lot on my mind. Thank you for coming to get me. How did you know to come?"

"It's the strangest thing, really. Someone called me early this morning, a little after midnight, and told me to be at the hospital waiting for you at 2 p.m. He didn't explain more than that, and so, I took a chance and came." He reached over and squeezed his little girl's hand. "The thing is I have heard that voice before; I just can't place it, though."

Savanna debated then whether she should divulge the conversations she had with the same caller and thought better of it. *Daddy's been through enough. He still grieves from Mom's death, and I don't want to add to that by worrying him.*

"I'd like to stay with you a few days, if that's OK," Savanna said. "Just until I feel like my old self again. I'm not ready to go home and face Melissa yet."

"No problem, stay as long as you like," Gerald said. He was excited at the thought of having someone else in the house again. Things there felt so empty and sad since Mary Ellen died.

When they arrived at the house, Savanna followed Gerald inside and trailed behind him as he carried her things to the room she used as a little girl. It seemed smaller now, and she couldn't recall how many years it had been since she slept there.

"I'm just going to lie down a bit, Daddy. Then, maybe we can have some supper together," she said.

When Gerald was safely gone, Savanna turned on her laptop and waited impatiently for her browser to connect with an Internet signal. Then, she typed in the address the caller gave her, holding her breath as the page loaded.

A cheery yellow screen greeted her by name. *Welcome home, Savanna. When you're ready, click <u>here</u>.* She clicked the hyperlink dutifully.

A screen with a black background opened in a new window.

Three columns stretched down the page, filled with filenames in tiny fonts and white script. She was puzzled. What were these files?

She began to open them, one by one. They were records, of all types, from several sources. Over the next few minutes, a pattern emerged. Some files were prefixed with the letters ME—for Mary Ellen—and some with S—for Sue, Savanna's grandmother. The sources presented in the files were exhaustive, and Savanna wondered how anyone could have pulled them all together in one place.

There were medical files, files from the mental health hospital, police records, autopsy reports, and psychiatric evaluations for both her mother and grandmother. Knowing it would take hours to read them, she quietly turned the lock on her bedroom door to ensure she wouldn't be disturbed, curled up under the quilt on her bed, handmade by her grandmother, and started reading.

Three hours later, she heard a quiet knock on her door, and then, her father's voice.

"Vanny? Care to wake up for some dinner? I made your favorite—meatloaf and mashed potatoes."

"Be right there, Dad," Savanna said, wiping tears from her face.

It was heart wrenching to read the documents about her dead mother and grandmother, but more than being sad at the task of wading through the paper trail their lives had left, she was confused and scared.

There was more information in the documents than she expected, and it would take time to process it all, but two things stuck out to her and needled at her conscious mind, like wayward straws sticking out of a new, perfect straw hat, scratchy and bothersome.

The police records for both Sue and Mary Ellen cited suicide as the cause of death, and the coroners' reports corroborated this; yet, a strange, cryptic comment in the coroners' reports bothered her. In Sue's report, the coroner hand-scribbled a note at the bottom, as if it were an afterthought: "Death by strangulation is apparent. Evidence of struggle, abrasions on wrists and arms, is curious." On

Mary Ellen's report, there was a similar note: "A preponderance of evidence suggests self-inflicted asphyxiation; blunt force trauma to head is also noted, though the timing of this wound cannot be pinpointed."

Perhaps even more disturbing was the psychiatric evaluation on both Sue and Mary Ellen. Sue's evaluation was completed years before her death, and Mary Ellen's evaluation was completed shortly after Sue's death. Both referred to a name Savanna never heard of, and the note to each file was the same:

Patient has genetic predisposition for Munchausen Syndrome, reference convicted serial killer Mary Ellen Tanning, inmate #45112 in Washington State Penitentiary, a genetic relative of the patient. — Dr. Spence, Chief of Staff, Cut Bank Municipal Psychiatric Hospital

Savanna shut down her laptop and stumbled from her bedroom. Her head was a jumble of thoughts, none comforting. She was told as a small girl that her grandmother committed suicide, and she knew her mother blamed herself for that. Her father told her that her mother committed suicide, and Dr. Spence suggested Mary Ellen was upset in the days before by the revelation about Savanna's sexuality. Yet, both women died similarly, and with additional injuries besides strangulation. *A coincidence?* Savanna wondered.

Gerald set a steaming plate in front of her, and her stomach lurched with hunger.

"I didn't know you could cook, Daddy," she said.

Gerald blushed. "Well, honestly, I haven't had to. The neighbor ladies have kept me fed and the freezer stocked."

"May I ask you a question?"

"Sure," Gerald mumbled, shoveling a spoonful of potatoes into his mouth.

"Did Mom or Grandma ever talk about a relative named Mary Ellen Tanning?"

"Tanning... Tanning... Tanning..." Gerald thought long and hard. "No, can't say I've ever heard that name."

"And what about Munchausen Syndrome? Ever heard of it?"

"Nope, never have. What is it?"

"It's nothing, really. Truly, it's nothing. It's where patients make up illnesses trying to get attention. It's a mental disorder. You don't suppose Mom had that, do you?"

Gerald looked down at his plate, and Savanna sensed she had pushed too hard with her questions. It was too much, too soon.

"I honestly don't know, Vanny. Your mom was sick with many things—mostly grief and guilt. I didn't know Sue, so I can't say what might have ailed her. All I know is Dr. Spence has been an attentive, eager physician to our family for years, first to your mom and to your grandmother before her. If this syndrome were something that runs in the family, he would know about it. Why don't you talk to him and ask?"

No, I don't think I will, Daddy, Savanna thought. I'm not interested in being locked up and drugged again. The man stole three months of my life from me in the name of psychiatric healing, and I think it's time to break the cycle and find a new family doctor.

CHAPTER 19

When will Mama come home?

—Colton

Melissa unlocked the door of the apartment she shared with Savanna, cradling a sack of groceries in one hand and a sleeping three-year-old in the other. It was a wonder she didn't drop both, but Melissa wasn't prone to dropping things. She was highly competent, physically strong, and always on top of her game.

Gingerly setting down the brown paper bag on the kitchen counter, she gingerly readjusted Colton's sleeping body more and walked back toward his bedroom to tuck him in. As she passed by the phone in the living room, she allowed herself a quick glance at the phone cradle. The lack of a flashing light indicated, again, there were no new messages, and she frowned.

"Good night, sweet pea," she crooned, tucking the small boy under a nest of blankets. "Mommy loves you."

Colton stirred slightly in his dreams, and his eyes fluttered open briefly. "Where is Mama?" he asked. "When will Mama come home?"

To Colton, Melissa was Mommy, and Savanna was Mama, and he continued to struggle with Mama's absence. Melissa struggled, too, with finding the right words to explain that Mama was sick, that she didn't know when Mama was coming home, and to herself, that she hadn't heard from Savanna in several months.

"There, there, little love. You rest now; get some sleep," she said, ruffling his hair and patting his back until he finally fell back asleep.

Leaving her abusive husband, Colton's father, was difficult, but wondering when her girlfriend would come home was infinitely more difficult. She thought back to the days of living with Peter, the fights they had and the way he didn't seem to even be aware that they shared a newborn son. Fatherhood grows on some men, but it didn't grow on Peter.

He started drinking more, coming home later and later, if at all, and when he started hitting her, Melissa knew it was time to leave. To her family and friends, it was an understandable conclusion to reach, and they supported her. But they didn't understand the source of her fear, not really. Although everyone thought she left because she was tired of being hit, Melissa knew her fear was different. She was afraid of hitting back, and when she did hit back, she feared she wouldn't be able to control herself.

She was a state-champion wrestler and the primal urge to fight never left her. With each of Peter's blows to her head, her back, her face, she felt herself reawakening what her wrestling coach called "beast mode." What would happen if she fought him off the next time he struck? Would she crack his skull, go too far, and kill him? Then, what would happen to Colton? She couldn't allow herself to stay and find out, so she left.

When she met Savanna at a charity 5k race, the floor fell out from under her and with it, all the pent-up frustration, hurt, disappointment, and doubt caused by her marriage to Peter fell away. With Savanna, she felt whole again, safe again, and the angry beast inside her, awakened when Peter was in her life, fell back to sleep.

She poured herself a glass of wine and settled on the couch, making note of the time—9:00 P.M. Her shift at the hospital ran several hours long, thanks to an emergency surgery she was called in to help with, and she was grateful her babysitter was amenable to

Colton staying a little longer. It was, of course, regrettable that she missed the evening with her small son.

She thought again about Colton's nightly question about Mama. He was right—they were both worried, both missing her, both wondering when she would come home. 9:00 P.M.—it was too late to call the hospital, but she decided to, anyway.

She dialed the number, as she did every night for more than two months. Her call rang into the nurse's station, and to her surprise, someone new answered the phone.

"This is Esther; how may I help?"

"Esther? Oh, um, I was looking for Nelly. Is she around?" Melissa asked.

"No, I'm sorry, ma'am, but Nelly no longer works here. Today was her last day. Is there something I can do?"

"Maybe. I call every night and get an update on my partner, a patient named Savanna, and Esther usually gives me that. Can you tell me how Savanna's doing?"

"Are you family?"

"I'm her girlfriend."

"Are you married?"

"No."

"I'm so sorry; I won't be able to help in that case." To her credit, Esther sounded genuine and sympathetic as she delivered this news.

Melissa wasn't too surprised by this response. When she tried to visit Savanna, she was told she had no rights to visit because their relationship was a domestic partnership, not a marriage. It was frustrating, but she knew the lack of rights of homosexual couples, and this was just the way the world worked.

"It's OK; I understand. I expected that . . ."

"Wait," the nurse interrupted. "Did you say Savanna?"

"I did, yes. She's been there for months."

"I ask because this is my first shift here, and I spent the better part of the evening reviewing every patient file, and there isn't a patient here by that name," Esther said.

"Oh, really? That's interesting. Can you check to see if she was discharged?"

"I'm sorry, ma'am, that's probably already more information than I should have shared. I wish you the best." The phone went dead.

Melissa took a long swig of her wine. *Savanna isn't there? If she were discharged, wouldn't I be the first person to know?*

She rinsed her glass and headed for bed, knowing it would be another fitful night. If she didn't have a sleeping boy in the room next door, she would have grabbed her keys and gone for a drive, checking for Savanna's car at her father's house, at the local hotels, at the bars they used to enjoy going to together, or any other place she could think to look. Sometimes, she wondered if she were too much, too obsessive, or if this was just what true love felt like.

CHAPTER 20

I would hate for you to choose an unauthentic lifestyle;
that can be so draining, you know?

—*Savanna's counsellor*

It had been a week since Savanna walked out of the mental hospital, and every day, she felt stronger. Her father was as attentive as he could be, giving her plenty of latitude for rest and keeping her fed and well nourished. He took care of everything—fielding calls for her from her employer ("She has gone through quite a bit of turmoil losing her mother; no, I don't know when she'll be able to come back to work. Yes, I'll tell her you called."), reactivating her cell phone, and paying her bills. He asked for nothing in return.

Savanna confined herself to her room, reading and rereading the extraordinarily thorough documentation her midnight caller provided. She couldn't help wondering who the source of it was and how someone could have compiled such detailed information in one place. She knew this was a herculean feat because she tried to access many of the same records—from the hospital, the coroner's office, and the police station—several years ago and met resistance every way she turned. She didn't have the "right clearance," the files "couldn't be found," or the person she needed to talk to about accessing the files was "out of town, with no known return date." Eventually, she gave up.

Now, at her fingertips, she had every file she ever imagined could possibly exist about her mother's and grandmother's deaths.

After a week of craning and straining her eyes reading small font on a digital screen, she was disappointed that she couldn't reach any conclusions about the suspicious nature of her loved ones' deaths. Outside the coroners' reports, the psychiatric diagnosis of Munchausen Syndrome, and the apparent relatedness to a convicted serial killer serving a life sentence for, not one, but fourteen coldblooded murders, she could make little sense from it all. Only one conclusion was prominent—she suspected her mother and grandmother did not commit suicide.

At the same time, the issues in their lives leading up to their deaths were still real to her—her grandmother was apparently a bigot; her mother was apparently a xenophobe.

Although she had no real leads or even foggy ideas about who could be so callous to help her grandmother and mother to their deaths, one fact remained—their deaths couldn't be changed, but she still had an opportunity to right an issue that caused her mother extreme distress before she died.

This was sealed by her father's insistence that she speak with a counsellor by phone, anonymously, to better understand a hereditary predisposition for Munchausen Syndrome, and the information she received in that counselling session. She called looking for validation that she didn't have it, especially because she couldn't remember seeing a doctor as an adult or even thinking about seeing one. However, Mary Ellen took her to physicians several times a year as a child, convinced she had certain ailments, and this caused Savanna to question whether she could expect the same behavior from herself someday, if she had kids.

After a brief chat with the counsellor, however, she left the call convinced more than ever that she did have Munchausen Syndrome. What convinced her? It was the counsellor's information on homosexuality that changed her thinking.

"Do you recall having a psychiatric assessment during your

formative years while you were in the care of your mother?" the counsellor asked.

"Yes, I remember having one. I was in middle school, and I chose to go to our homecoming dance with some girlfriends instead of the neighbor boy who asked me. He was strange, and I didn't feel comfortable on a date with him, so I went with the girls. The next Monday, my mom dragged me down to Dr. Spence's office for a sexuality assessment, and she pointed out to him that she suspected he would find I am a lesbian.

"I'm not certain what the results of his assessment were. I just remember being mortified by some questions he asked and angry with my mom for blowing something like a homecoming dance out of proportion. For months after, she referred to my 'condition' and make insidious comments about my life as a lesbian. I was so offended, so horrified, so hurt by that."

"And now? How would you categorize your sexual orientation now, Savanna?"

Savanna thought of Melissa, her only female partner, and the frustrating few relationships she had with men before meeting Melissa.

"I am in a relationship with a woman. Or, I should say, I was."

"It's probably too soon to tell whether you have the same Munchausen symptoms your mother and grandmother did, Savanna, but be watchful of symptoms surfacing. They can sometimes be exacerbated by stressful, straining, insecurity-inducing events in our life, bringing forward latent Munchausen tendencies.

"And one last thing, Savanna—you mentioned you were in a homosexual relationship, and I sensed some emotion there that I couldn't discern as sadness or relief. Consider carefully whether you truly relate to having a female partner, or whether this is simply something you have accepted blindly about yourself because of your mother's insistence that it is so. I would hate for you to choose a lifestyle that isn't authentic; that can be so draining, you know?"

She thanked the counsellor then and ended the call. Combined with everything she learned about her mother's death and the angst her mother experienced before her passing, Savanna could not escape the feeling of being responsible somehow for her death. It grieved her.

She thought about Melissa regularly, and though she missed her, she was hurt that Melissa never came to see her in the hospital.

"Dad?" Savanna asked at dinner that night.

"Mmmm?" he muttered between bites of tuna casserole, courtesy of the neighbor around the corner.

"Has anyone called for me besides the school? Like Melissa, perhaps?"

Gerald thought about it. "No, I can't think of anyone else who has. There was a call in the middle of the night, but I didn't get to the phone in time, and when I did, the caller had hung up. And that's about it. The phone has been quiet. Why, not even Dr. Spence has called. You know, to check up on you. Don't you find that strange?"

Considering the circumstances under which she released herself from the hospital, no, she didn't find this strange. Her Dad's response solved it, in her mind. Melissa didn't visit the hospital; Melissa didn't call. Clearly, they were through.

"Oh! I do remember a caller. I'm sorry; I forgot to tell you. I honestly don't know how I forgot. It was just yesterday evening. You went to take a bath, and then, I was asleep when you were done, and I forgot to write you a note."

"Who was it?" Savanna asked.

"A Detective Gray from the police station. He asked you to call him as soon as possible."

Savanna's heart skipped a beat. Drugged or not, half asleep or not, there was simply no way she could forget the handsome, blue-eyed cop who sat at her bedside for months. She noted mentally to call him back first thing in the morning.

CHAPTER 21

It gets worse, John.

—Midnight Caller

"I'm sorry for your loss, John."

"Detective Gray, so sorry to hear . . ."

"If I can help in any way, I'm here for you, John."

"So sorry, Detective."

A symphony of condolences followed Detective Gray to his desk on the first day back in the office after his Mediterranean vacation, followed by funeral leave. He was numb to them all by now—all the well wishes and kind thoughts—as his wife's family was in town for weeks, giving him the same lines and hoping they would be of comfort to him. They weren't.

Someone could say few things after your spouse's death that could comfort you and fewer things when your spouse's death seemed least likely to happen to your young family. One minute, they were enjoying a seaside, candlelit, private dinner for two and watching the sunset. The next thing he knew, she was choking and gagging, falling out of her chair, and rolling in the sand trying to breathe.

He rushed to her side, tried the Heimlich maneuver unsuccessfully, screamed for help, and he was there as she took her last breath several moments later. The resort staff did everything they could to revive her, but to no avail. She was gone, a week and a half into the most luxurious, most romantic, most sensual vacation he and his wife ever took.

How could she be there one minute, looking stunning in a shimmery, gold evening gown, and dead the next? How was he supposed to raise their daughter without her? How was he supposed to carry on back at home in Cut Bank? Would he ever breathe normally again without being gripped by a sudden rush of tears and grief? How could he retain his high-pressure job as Cut Bank's newest detective when all he wanted to do was crawl in a hole and die?

His grief was debilitating and, thankfully, the Chief gave him as much time off as he needed to put his wife's affairs in order and begin to work through healing. He was amazed at how accommodating the Chief was, especially when he'd already been gone from the office for two weeks on vacation. Surely, he was needed back at work, wasn't he? Who would take care of his job in his absence?

He tried to put these fears to rest, focusing instead on burying his wife, getting through the funeral, spending extra time with his daughter and his wife's family, and getting used to a new routine that didn't include the love of his life. He still didn't sleep well at night, which is understandable when you are present to witness your wife's passing and are powerless to do anything about it.

About a week after his late wife's family left town, he lay awake in his bed nursing a tumbler of scotch, his fourth to be exact, and the phone rang. It was close to midnight, a strange hour for a legitimate call, and he rushed to answer it before the ringing awoke his sleeping daughter.

"John Gray here," he said in a quiet, tipsy voice.

"John, please don't hang up. I'm a friend. I need to speak with you," a man's voice said.

Curious, John clicked on the tape recorder attached to his

phone's charging unit, just in case this was part of a case he learned about the day he returned to work.

"Who is this?" he asked.

"I can't identify myself just now, but please know I mean you no harm. I am deeply sorry for your loss, my most sincere condolences to you, but that is not the purpose of my call," the man said, and John struggled to identify where he heard that voice before. He checked the caller ID, but the display read that it was an unlisted number.

"Thank you for that. So, what is the purpose of your call exactly?" John pressed.

"I need to tell you two things. First, we've spoken before. Do you remember? You helped me several months ago when I asked for some case files. Only, my voice was disguised as a woman then. I told you I was calling from the insurance office."

"I remember," John said. It was a strange call, but he decided to help the caller because she seemed legitimate, and she asked for police records to investigate what she said was a case of insurance fraud. New to his position, he didn't think much more of it, and he was flattered to be called for help by someone as important as the vice president of Thrivent Health Insurance Company. When he asked her which files she needed, he made up his mind immediately. They were the records of a family he wanted to help. "Yes, I sent the files on Sue Pearson and her daughter Mary Ellen and granddaughter Savanna. Is that what you mean?"

"Yes, exactly. Very good, I'm glad you remember."

"So, what is this about then? What's the second thing you need to tell me?" Something told John he should stop recording this call. He stopped the recording device and hit the delete key to discard the audio file.

"The second thing won't be as easy to explain, but I need you to bear with me, John. Are you sitting?"

"Yes."

"Good. As I said, I understand you lost your wife recently. And I'm sorry about that."

"It was an accident, so there's really nothing to be sorry about, but I appreciate your thoughts," John said, speaking the words he spoke hundreds of times in the past month, as if on autopilot.

"Yes, yes, an accident. That is what you are meant to believe. What if I told you an autopsy was done on your wife?"

"I wouldn't believe you. I didn't authorize that."

"No, you didn't authorize it, but an autopsy was done, just the same. It's a standard protocol in the small Greek town where you stayed, just due course. Anyway, the autopsy report is in front of me now, and I need you to know what it says. Your wife didn't choke. Your wife was poisoned. The cause of death was asphyxiation because of a lethal level of succinylcholine."

John knew what succinylcholine was. He, of course, was a homicide detective.

"That doesn't make sense. She wasn't injected with it; we were alone there on the beach."

"Yes, you were, except for the waiter, who wasn't a resort waiter at all. He works for someone you know, someone you know well. Do you know Mark Crew?"

John dropped the phone and reached for the nearest wastebasket, finding it just in time to vomit three tumblers of whiskey and a slice of frozen pizza he ate at dinner.

"John? John, are you there?"

He heard the voice speaking from the dropped receiver, but couldn't stop vomiting long enough to grab it. Finally, after he regained his composure, he lifted the receiver once more.

"I'm back. Sorry. Sick."

"I understand; that's why I waited. Look, I know this is coming to you as a surprise, and I am sympathetic to what this must feel like—"

"Thanks," John said weakly. "You're telling me my wife was murdered. But why?"

"It's because of Savanna, I think," the caller said.

"Savanna? What does she have to do with this?" He recalled the beautiful girl the Chief instructed him to watch over in the mental hospital, the one with the gorgeous green eyes who was heartbroken to hear he was leaving for the Mediterranean.

"The files you gave me on her mother, her grandmother, and her were marked for Deep Dive. You know the term?"

He did. Deep Dive was the Chief's phrase for files that no one would ever find again. They were turned over to the Chief, and there was no telling of what happened to them next. Did he keep them in his office, in a safe, or in the landfill? No one knew.

"You sent them to me hours before you left for the Mediterranean, hours before the Chief planned to Deep Dive them, and you left a record of having pulled the files to review them. The Chief wasn't too happy about that, obviously," the caller continued.

"So he killed my wife?" John could hardly believe pulling files warranted murder, but clearly, he didn't know his boss as well as he thought he did.

"It gets worse, John."

"How much worse?"

"You need to know that there are photographs of you leaning over your wife moments before she fell. They are incriminating. They look as though you injected something into her leg."

John thought back to those last precious moments he had with his wife.

"She dropped her napkin! Oh, my God! Her napkin fell, I leaned over to pick it up, and this is none of your business, but I trailed my finger up her calf and let it linger on her thigh before straightening again."

"Yes, regardless, the Chief has this picture. He also has the cause of death report. I just want you to know so you can be careful. Do everything he says, don't cross him in any way, or I think you'll be facing indictment and extradition to Greece."

"Thanks," John said weakly, another wave of vomit threatening to rise to the top.

"I'll be in touch. I'm here to help," the caller said. The line went dead.

CHAPTER 22

Tell the whole truth; tell it all!

—Three crows in a cemetery

"I need to tell you something, Mama," Savanna said, kneeling in the grass at the foot of her mother's grave. A breeze ruffled her skirt then, and she took it as a sign her mother was there, listening patiently.

"I know I haven't visited in a while, but it's because I've waited for something to share, something that would make you happy. I know I haven't made you happy. That is, I haven't made you happy. I tried, but—"

This was precisely why she didn't come to visit her mother, she realized then. Even in death, her relationship with her mother was rocky, and she never thought she said the right things.

She sighed. *I'd better just get right to the point, make this quick, and get out of here. Maybe it'll get easier in time, visiting her. Today is a first try; that's all.*

"I was in the hospital a long time, Mom. After you died, I was depressed. Then, I think I was depressed even longer than usual because of the medications they put me on, but someone helped me. Someone helped me see I was sedated, and helped me get out of the hospital. I probably don't make much sense, but I also got more information about Grandma and you. It's a lot of stuff, I'm unsure what it all means, and I don't know whether any of it even matters now.

"What I do know is, before you died, you were upset with me about being a lesbian. And that's not what I want to talk about with you, not really, because I don't think we'll ever see eye-to-eye on that, but here's what I do want to say—I haven't seen Melissa in a year, and I think she has moved on. And I've been dating again, and this time I'm dating men. I thought you'd like to hear that.

"I found this online dating site, and I met some nice men. Dad met them all before we went out. I insisted on it. Losing you has been so difficult on the family, and I just didn't know for a long while whether I could trust my instincts anymore. So, Dad helped me and kept an eye on whom I was going out with. It made him feel useful, and I think he needs that now, and it made me feel safe.

"There's one guy I've been seeing for six months or so now, Mom. I think you'd really like him. He has a little girl. She's a little girl over a year old, and she's the cutest thing. His wife died unexpectedly, and I guess we both need each other after what we've been through.

"Anyway, Dad really loves him. He's been over to the house for dinner. We take his little girl to the park, to the zoo, and the beach, and it feels good. He makes me very happy.

"I still live with Dad, Mom. We get along really well, better than ever, but we still miss you. I haven't told him yet, or anyone really, but the guy I'm seeing—John Gray—asked me to move in with him. And Mom? I can't believe I'm even saying this aloud, but I have to practice sharing the news, don't I? I . . . Mom, I . . . I think I'm pregnant, Mom.

"You're going to be a grandma. I thought you'd want to know."

Savanna looked at her mother's gravestone, wishing she could see her mother's face, instead of cold granite. Sharing her news felt anticlimactic somehow, and she was certain the cemetery venue was to blame.

Three crows landed on a branch over her head; the sound of

their ebony, heavy wings startled her. They cawed mercilessly as if to say, "Tell the whole truth; tell it all!"

So, with a sigh, she did. "I'm excited to be a mother, and I really love John. I know you'd like him too. And I know you would be happy to know I'm with a man now, not a woman. But the truth is, I still think of Melissa. And for Colton, I miss him too. But I know it's better this way, for me to be with John, and I know that would have made you happy. I don't want to live my life with someone who makes me wonder whether I'm disappointing my mother somehow."

As soon as she finished speaking, the crows left the branch overhead, as if pleased with her honest confession, and she stood to leave.

"I'll be busy in my new life, Mama. But I'll come back and visit you again soon; I promise."

CHAPTER 23

It was disgusting, really, the way the Mayor and his cronies behaved.

—Brandon

Since the year he accepted the Cut Bank Town Council seat, Brandon was busy. As suspected, his willingness to sit on the Council and vote according to Mayor Roy Travis' agenda rewarded him with a distiller's license and the approval of his rezoning request. He was finally close to obtaining the business loan he needed to open his brewery downtown, and it was an exciting time in his life.

Between Council work, the coffee shop, and making plans for his new business, Brandon fell into a deep sleep every night. He couldn't even recall the last time he had nightmares about the past and, even better, he couldn't recall the last time he needed a sleeping pill from Dr. Spence to get him through the night. By all accounts, life was good. At least, it seemed to be.

Except it wasn't, not really. When his busyness stopped long enough for him to catch his breath and be honest with himself, quite a few things were awry in his world, and he wasn't sure how to deal with them.

The older he got, the more alone he felt, for one thing. Feeling alone made him think of Mary Ellen, his first love. He missed her, even the cantankerous middle-aged version of the sweet girl he fell for decades ago. He knew she would be proud of him for following his dream to open his business. While at the same time, she would have been angry as hell that it was a brewery, and for some odd reason, he missed her for not being there to respond and give him grief for leading Cut Bank into the pit of moral decay, as she would likely have put it. She had been the white to his black, the female to his male, and the clouds on his sunny day and, in so many ways, he now missed the yin to his yang.

It didn't help that, even now, a year after her death, people still badmouthed Mary Ellen as if she were alive, as if she were still just up the street on her computer creating havoc and rabble-rousing on her social media sites. In every Council meeting he was in, for example, her name came up. It was as if Dr. Spence, Mark Crew, and Mayor Travis couldn't let her rest in peace.

Her name came up as the butt of their jokes. ("You're not pulling a 'Mary Ellen,' are you, Doctor?" meant, "You're not really going to argue with me, are you?") Her name came up when they had something to hide. ("Careful buying that boat, Mayor, Mary Ellen will have it all over social media by suppertime and make some crazy accusation about using taxpayer money to buy it!" And, of course, that's precisely where the Mayor's boat came from.) Her name came up when they plotted to exploit their positions in ways that benefitted them. ("I have the proposition on seizing the property on 4th and Main for my new liquor store, and I think you'll find it's been Mary-Ellen-proofed. No voter will see through it for what it is—a tax write-off," Mark Crew said recently.)

It was really disgusting, the way the Mayor and his cronies behaved. Brandon had more than he could stand of their conniving, plotting, and finagling, and he was ready to resign. He didn't want to be around it anymore, but at the same time, he also recognized how much trouble the three kings could make for him if he left Council without their blessing.

Every day, he thought through his options for expunging himself from Council. Every day, an exit strategy that wouldn't ruin him eluded him.

Then, there was Gerald. If missing Mary Ellen and annoyance with the Mayor and Company were already bad enough, the sight of Gerald never failed to send Brandon spiraling into further depths of despair.

The man looked like a ghost. Once portly and well fed, Gerald was but a shell of himself these days. He looked as though he never slept, as though he was racked with grief, and as though there was no one in the world to look after him. On top of that, he was broke.

Whereas, Gerald used to come to the coffee shop and order a fancy latte and a half-dozen muffins to go, he came in these days with his own mug ($0.10 discount automatically) and ordered the house drip ($0.79), the money for which he counted out in nickels, dimes, and pennies. He still had his house, and he still had his job, but he was also a bit quite out of money paying off Mary Ellen's funeral and Savanna's hospital bills.

"I thought Mary Ellen had a life insurance policy. Didn't she, Gerald?" Brandon asked that morning when Gerald came in looking a little grayer than usual.

"She did," he said, counting out pennies on the countertop. "Half her money went to Savanna, who signed it over to some legal office I never heard of over in Willow Bend, and the rest . . . Well, it's the strangest thing. There was a document signing over the rest to Phil Gravy, signed in Mary Ellen's hand before she died, years ago. In fact. I tried to call Phil, but I think he moved, and I have seen no one around town who knows how to reach him. He didn't even come to her funeral. So, I just plod along, trying to make ends meet one month at a time. I can't do much about any of it."

"I didn't know all that, Gerald. I'm sorry," Brandon said.

Gerald waved his comment aside. "It's not your fault. I just wonder sometimes . . ."

"What do you wonder?" Brandon pressed.

"I shouldn't; I know I shouldn't. I just can't help wondering whether Mary Ellen didn't kill herself and whether someone was after her insurance money. I don't know. It keeps me up at night, honestly—the wondering."

"I have things I wonder about too. I understand."

Brandon put his hand over Gerald's hand, and Gerald's fingers froze in the middle of counting his coins. He looked into Gerald's tired eyes and offered a sincere smile.

"I can't bring Mary Ellen back to you, and I don't have answers to the things you wonder about, but there is one small thing I can do, if you'll let me."

"Go on," Gerald said.

"When you step into this shop, your order is always on me; in a few months, when you step into my brewery, your order will always be on me. Please, let me do this small thing for you. I miss her, too, you know. And in some small way, looking out for you makes me feel I'm doing something she'd be happy about," he said.

"For a change," Gerald laughed, and Brandon joined in.

"Yeah, I know, right? Seemed like I never did anything right by Mary Ellen," Brandon laughed.

"Then, I accept," Gerald smiled. "Thank you. If it makes Mary Ellen happy wherever she is, I'm all about that, and if it pisses her off, my taking gifts from you, well, I'm all about that too. She was quite a girl, never easy to please, and I miss her. You cheered me up today, just by letting me know you miss her too."

CHAPTER 24

Next of kin is someone named Gerald, and the insurer's name is John Gray.

—Asan Patel

Melissa did not move on. Each month that passed without hearing from Savanna was worse than the prior one, and Colton still asked about her. Before Savanna's mother died, Melissa tried to learn more about Savanna's family; Savanna never wanted to talk about her parents, though, except in generalities. She feared her mother would be unaccepting of their relationship, and she wasn't ready at that time to rock the boat.

Now, Melissa wished she pressed for more information. She didn't even know the name of Savanna's father, and Savanna's cell phone number was disconnected.

Savanna hadn't been back to work since being discharged from the hospital, and she didn't frequent their usual haunts any longer. Melissa knew this because she looked for Savanna everywhere regularly.

One night, she thought she saw Savanna out of the corner of her eye, stepping into a truck's passenger side. The man holding the door for her was smiling and clearly smitten with his female companion. When he leaned in for a kiss before walking around the truck to the driver's side, Melissa dismissed the romance unfolding before her eyes. *That couldn't have been Savanna. Savanna doesn't kiss men.*

Despite her heightened awareness of the people in her surrounding area, always keeping her eyes trained for a glimpse of Savanna, and a deep longing to run into Savanna again, she grew less and less hopeful as the months passed. Then, twelve months after her discharge from the hospital, Savanna resurfaced in Melissa's life, or at least, her name did.

As a surgical tech at Cut Bank's medical center, Melissa didn't have much visibility into the patient side of things outside the surgical department. The medical center encompassed a hospital and a clinical setting as well, including a family medicine practice and several subspecialty medical offices.

Asan Patel played volleyball with Melissa on Wednesday evenings, and the two struck up a friendship. In exchange for helping Asan work on his serve, Asan agreed to help Melissa by periodically checking the medical records for the hospital system, in case Savanna's name popped up. He didn't have access to query her demographics, but if her name came up as part of a new billing transaction, he could tie into her patient registrar information. So far, all was quiet on that front for months.

When Melissa's cell phone rang at 6:00 a.m. on her way to drop off Colton at the sitter's house, she nearly didn't answer it. The caller ID showed the hospital's main number, and she was resistant to take a call from work during her last few precious moments with her son. Something prompted her to answer, though.

"Melissa? It's Asan. Sorry, I know it's early."

"It sure is, but not a problem. What's up?" Melissa asked. Asan never called her; they saved their chatting for the volleyball court. What was this all about?

"Your girl came through the ER last night, and I thought you'd want to know."

"Savanna?"

"Yes."

"What can you tell me?" Melissa asked, her heart beginning to race.

"I don't have perfect visibility into the visit, but it looks as though she came in complaining of abnormal bleeding. Her discharge diagnosis was complications of pregnancy."

"Pregnancy? Are you kidding me? Are you sure you have the right person?"

"Yes, there's no doubt about it. Her date of birth matches the one you gave me."

Melissa didn't know how to respond, and she wasn't even sure she could. It seemed preposterous that Savanna could be pregnant.

"Oh, I have one more piece of info for you," Asan said, interrupting her thoughts. "I have her home address and phone number. Next of kin is someone named Gerald, and the insurer's name is John Gray."

"Thank you, Asan. Could you e-mail it to me? I'm driving. See you Wednesday and thanks again."

Melissa called in to work and said she'd be late, then proceeded to drive around the block repeatedly while Colton slept in his car seat, and her mind sped at the speed of light. She needed time to think.

It wasn't the news she expected to hear that day, or ever. Confusion gave way to disbelief, disbelief gave way to hurt, and hurt gave way in short order to anger. Anger was an unhealthy emotion for Melissa, as were feelings of betrayal. Yet, she couldn't deny she felt a mix of the two, and they were intertwined, taking on a life of their own and synergistically growing stronger by the minute.

CHAPTER 25

*. . . the words were of the type
that could never be unread.*

—*Savanna*

"Just rest, baby," John said, kissing Savanna's hair. "The doctor said you're on bed rest for a week until all spotting stops."

"I know; I just don't do well sitting still," she replied.

They were curled up on the couch in the living room of the home Savanna shared with her father, and Gerald was away at work. He offered to call in sick to work and stay home with her after their late night in the ER, but Savanna insisted she would be fine alone. Then, John came over on his lunch break to check on her, and it was nice to have company.

"Do you think the baby will be OK?" Savanna asked, curling up in John's arms and enjoying the comfort of having him near. She had a pang of guilt, as she did nearly every time she recognized how much she enjoyed John's quiet, masculine strength, and her mind drifted to Melissa. She wondered where she was, what she was doing, and why she never called.

"Yes, I think everything will be fine. The ultrasound looked good, and we have a healthy baby girl growing stronger every day. Soon, Lucy will be a big sister. She's already so excited."

"Have you thought of any names you like? I've toyed with Meg, as in M-E-G for Mary Ellen and Gerald. But it seems selfish to name our daughter after my parents. What have you come up with?"

John didn't have a chance to answer. His radio beeped, and the sound of dispatch could be heard breaking in, crackling an announcement.

"Need all units to report to East High School. A suspected shooter was reported in the parking lot. Repeat. A suspected shooter at East High School. All units report."

John stood up from the couch, kissing the top of Savanna's head.

"Duty calls. Gotta go, baby. Anything you need before I scoot?"

"Yes, actually, if you have time, there's a box in my mom's closet. There's not much left in there, but I remember seeing her first-aid box on the floor, just inside the door. I think there's a heating pad in there still. Could you run and grab it for me?" Savanna asked.

"Sure thing," he said and walked toward the bedroom and Mary Ellen's old closet.

She leaned back into the sofa and took a long drink from her water bottle. *John is so kind, so good, and so attentive. I'm fortunate to have him, and I'm excited to be having our baby. Melissa is in my past, and that's all there is to it,* she thought, trying to resolve her feelings of guilt once more and for the last time.

John reappeared moments later. He knew the closet well, and he was in it once before. It still gave him the creeps to think about seeing Mary Ellen swinging from the closet ceiling and the command the Chief gave him to have Savanna—his Savanna—taken into custody that night. So much changed since then, and it all seemed surreal how far they had come together and how much they helped each other heal.

The last time he was in the closet, though, it was filled with clothing, shoes, and boxes, and because the Chief told him exactly what to look for to complete his investigation, he didn't paw around too much. Still, it didn't take him long to locate the box Savanna described; there really wasn't much left in the closet, except disturbing memories.

"Baby, I brought the first-aid kit and, not sure if I should have intruded, but it sat on top of a book that looked pretty old. Thought I'd bring that too. You'll know what to do with it. Gotta go," he said. "See you tonight. Oh—and don't leave that couch! Doctor's orders!"

Savanna nodded, accepting the first-aid kit and book. The heating pad quickly located, she plugged it in next to the couch and settled into it, already feeling the tension in her back begin to unwind. Picking up the book, she studied it curiously.

It was a journal, clearly—the kind of blank book in which her mother used to love to scribble. When her mother died, Savanna couldn't locate any of the various books her mother wrote in over the years, which was curious and surprising to her. But with so many other things going on in her life then, she didn't think much more about it. It was odd that this one resurfaced in such a strange location; but then, she couldn't recall that anyone thought to look under the large, white metal first-aid kit. It was left, instead, in its place, in the place it always was for as long as Savanna could remember—just inside the door of her mother's closet.

She touched the front cover delicately. The worn leather cover was soft, and a black cord bound the book. She unfastened it, opened to the first page, and began to read. Her heart raced, and she shut the book. She didn't know whether she had the strength to read her mother's private thoughts, especially the ones in this volume, the beginning of which dated to exactly one year before her death.

She reopened the cover, flipped on to the light next to the couch, and placed her hand protectively on her belly. *Somehow, I think Mom would have wanted me to have this, to read this, to know what her last days were like,* Savanna thought.

So, she read, and the words were of the type that could never be unread.

CHAPTER 26

She's weeks away from giving me my first grandchild, and I want nothing more than to keep her and the baby safe.

—Gerald

"Gentlemen, thank you for meeting with me on such short notice," the Mayor said. "We have a problem. Doc, can you fill Mark in on what has transpired?"

"Absolutely," Doctor Spence said. "I was just leaving the coffee shop when Gerald entered. This was yesterday. He was in such a rush that I was immediately curious, so, instead of leaving, I ducked behind that short wall just inside the entrance and waited for a moment."

There was a tap on the sauna door, and the Mayor wrapped his towel more tightly around his waist before standing to answer it.

"No," he whispered through the door, impatiently. "We don't need anything at this time, but thank you."

To his friends, after returning to his seat, he explained, "The staff have changed around here, and I'm meeting with difficulty trying to train the new folks to understand that we don't want to be disturbed here. Stupid peasants. Go on, Doctor."

"Yes, well, anyway, Gerald rushed to the counter and said to

Brandon, 'She found it! Savanna found it! We thought it had gone missing, like the rest of her journals, but Savanna found Mary Ellen's journal, the one she kept right up until—' Then, Brandon shushed him and said, 'Not here, not now. It's not safe.'"

"That's impossible," Mark Crew said. "I saw to it that all her journals were confiscated from the house."

"Yes, we know; you told us that before, but did you look to make sure you got them all, including the most recent one?" the Mayor asked.

"Well, I told John Gray to have one of the guys verify dates were accounted for in the ones I picked up, so I assumed—"

"That's the problem, then," the Mayor interrupted. "You assumed. And now, God knows what Savanna has in her hands, what incriminating things she might already have read."

"You know; it's a shame that family is so cursed," Dr. Spence said. "First, Sue, then Mary Ellen, and now Savanna. Why can't those women manage to stay alive?"

"You know what to do, gentlemen," the Mayor said. "I have my bid for the governor's seat nearly cinched, and this is no time for unnecessary drama. Take care of it."

"You got it," Mark said, and Dr. Spence nodded his head in agreement.

Across town, another meeting was occurring. Off bed rest finally, Savanna took the evening to shop, and Gerald gathered his friends in her absence.

Over steaming mugs of coffee brought over in a large, stainless steel carafe from the coffee shop where Brandon worked, Gerald, Brandon, and John Gray settled into armchairs in the living room. It was not a peaceful settling, though, and all three men fidgeted and readjusted in their chairs.

"So, you've read it then, Gerald?" Brandon asked.

"Yes, and it changes everything," Gerald said, sipping from his steaming mug.

"How so?" asked John.

"Well, it seems Mary Ellen lived her last days in a lot of fear. She mentioned a book she couldn't seem to rid herself of, one with an image on the cover that disturbed her, and whenever she threw it out, it showed up again in odd places. From what she wrote, it drove her crazy, and I sort of always knew that, but something more seemed to bother her beyond the book, though she's not clear in her scribbles what exactly it was."

"Maybe if you tell us exactly what she said, we can help you decipher it," said John.

Gerald picked up the weathered leather journal and turned to the back, and one of the last few pages containing Mary Ellen's handwriting. He read aloud:

It's happening again. They're after me; I just know it. Appointment with Dr. Spence today, hopefully some new meds will help my anxiety. This is either real or happening to me, just as it did to Mom, or I'm having an episode, and it's all a figment of my imagination. Either way, I'm scared.

"What do you think she meant when she said it's happening again?" asked Brandon.

"That's the part that's puzzling me too. I think she's talking about her mom and how her mom lost control and killed herself. But then, I got this call last night around midnight, and it has me rethinking everything I thought I knew about Sue's and Mary Ellen's deaths," Gerald said.

"I got a call last night too," said Brandon.

"As did I, and it's not the first time," said John.

The three men looked at one another, disbelief on their faces.

"A man's voice, right?" asked Gerald.

"Yep. He said, 'It's going to happen again if you don't do

something. Open your eyes, and ask Savanna. She has all the proof you need,'" said Brandon.

"That's exactly what he said to me too," said John. Gerald nodded, as if to say, "Me too."

"I haven't seen Savanna today," John continued. "But I'll check in with her tonight when she gets back from shopping."

"Let us know what she says," said Brandon. "And for the record, I never believed for a minute that Mary Ellen or Sue committed suicide. I've just never been able, until now, to figure out who in the world would have been able to murder them both in such a similar fashion and cover their tracks so carefully. I think I'm starting to figure it out, though," he said, thinking of his Town Council experiences of late.

John thought about his wife choking and sputtering on the beach. His perception of how Cut Bank worked was starting to change as well.

"Let's meet again tomorrow evening," Gerald said. "Until then, help me keep an eye on Savanna, will you? She's weeks away from giving me my first grandchild, and I want nothing more than to keep her and the baby safe."

Little Mama was next to the pawnshop and so, saying she was shopping for the baby wasn't a complete lie. She spent a solid hour walking the aisles of Little Mama, admiring the baby clothes and bottles and even adding a few packages of diapers to her cart. That way, she was legitimately shopping for the baby, in case her dad or John asked.

With her meager purchase tucked in the car, she didn't head home right away. Instead, she walked into Five Star Pawn and proceeded immediately to the gun case at the back of the store. She was never around guns much in her life, but then, never in her life had she felt as insecure as she did now.

Mom's journal was clear. Something was up in the weeks and hours before she died, no doubt about it. She didn't crack and hang herself; she was trying to get help. She was going to the doctor's office that day, for Christ's sake. That's not the last action of a woman intent on killing herself, she thought, trying to make eye contact with the salesclerk across the store to indicate she was waiting for assistance.

He nodded at her, and she took that to mean he'd be right over, at least, eventually. She eyed the leggy, bleached blond with whom he flirted. On second thought, it might be a while.

Then, there were the mysterious phone calls. They were all hang-ups, but they unnerved her. Then, there was the car that kept driving slowly past her house; she'd seen it a dozen times. She wished her midnight caller would call again so she could get some answers, because hadn't he said he would help protect her?

Feeling as if you are losing your mind is frightening and Savanna spent several sleepless nights trying to make sense of what to do next. She had a baby on the way; she needed to protect herself more than ever.

She decided two things: one, it was time to take all data the midnight caller gave her and share it with her dad and with John. As much as she worried it would upset her father, she needed him to have all the facts so, together, they could figure out what happened to her mom. And John was an investigator, so he'd definitely know what to do. Two, she needed a gun. All alone in her dad's house all day meant she needed to protect herself.

"I'll take that one," she said to the clerk when he finally made it to the gun counter to assist her.

"That's a nice piece," he said. "I'd definitely feel better if my baby mama was packing a .380 handgun when I'm away."

"Perfect. That's exactly the one I want, then."

CHAPTER 27

Meet me at the hospital.

—Gerald

"John? Got a minute?" The Chief's voice on his work line jolted John out of the quagmire in his head. He was sending Savanna a text to check in on her and see whether she could start sleeping at his place for a while, for added protection. He also wanted to make sure they got some time together that day to go over whatever proof the midnight caller thought she might have.

"Sure, boss, I'll be right over," he replied and dutifully started walking toward the Chief's office.

John laid low the past year and a half since his wife died. He did exactly what he was told, but generally steered clear of the Chief. Thankfully, Mark hadn't needed him for much, and there hadn't been any requests from John for special favors or top-secret assignments, not since the night Mary Ellen died.

At the same time, he worked hard to keep his private life to himself. It would do him no good professionally or, he suspected, with his boss if people around the police station knew he was dating Savanna. He had arrested her, as instructed, and now, he was fathering her child. People would talk, and he didn't need talk. So far, he felt he was successful at keeping his job, staying below the radar, and not rocking the boat with the Chief. John felt his good luck was about to run out, though.

He knocked on the Chief's door gingerly, and he was ushered inside.

"Close the door, son," Mark said.

Yep, this is it. My luck has run out.

"Yes, sir," John said and sat directly across from the Chief.

"I'm going to need your help again, son."

John looked down at his hands, and his heartbeat was loud enough he heard it thudding in his ears.

"What? You've got cold feet, son? Your padded salary and disappearing mortgage, free gym membership, and new truck aren't enough for you anymore?"

Looking up, John cleared his throat and took a deep breath. "Everything's fine, sir. No problems at all. What can I do to help?"

"That's a good boy," Mark said. "I just need you to be on call for the next few nights, OK? Meaning, when I call you, you answer, and you follow my instructions exactly. Just like before. Got it?"

John didn't like the sound of this; it was too reminiscent of the night Mary Ellen died. If this was about Savanna, he might be able to use his position as the Chief's right-hand man to gather some intel and protect her.

"Something going down, Chief?" John asked, willing his voice to sound curious, but not too curious.

"Yes, something's going down, but that's all you need to know. Just stay close to your phone."

Mark wasn't going to budge on sharing information; that much was certain.

"No problem. Tell me again; what night will you need me? I just want to make sure I have everything settled so I can make myself available to you," John said.

"Tonight. Maybe tomorrow night, but probably tonight."

As he walked back to his desk, John frantically sent a text message to Gerald: *Something's going to happen. Can you get home to Savanna?*

Tied up all day in an in-service that annoyingly was a no-phone-zone, Gerald feigned interest in the speaker, but he was inwardly distracted. Savanna was on his mind, and he tried to tell himself she was fine. He pictured her lying peacefully in bed, as he saw her that morning when he left for work, resting and preparing for her impending journey into motherhood. He double-checked the doors were locked before leaving and that her phone was charged and within her reach. Again, he tried to tell himself she would be fine; everything would be fine.

Savanna slept late, until around noon, and woke feeling better rested than she had in a long time. Having her gun tucked under her pillow gave her the comfort she needed to rest well. She yawned and stretched, placed one hand on her belly to acknowledge her baby's soft kicks, and with her other hand, reached for her phone.

John tried to call several times, she noticed, and left a text message: *I need to know you're OK. Call me when you wake up.*

She got out of bed and went to the restroom, vowing to call John as soon as she got some coffee in her and felt more awake. She needed to arrange to see him that evening to talk about the files the midnight caller gave her access to, and she was sure he'd be agreeable to spending the evening with her. *I'll call him soon*, she thought and headed for the coffee pot.

Her trek to the kitchen was interrupted by the sound of the mail carrier dropping the mail in the box just outside the front door, and she changed course to retrieve it. Opening the front door, she gulped the fresh, vibrant air—the previous night's rain left her world feeling fresh and renewed, and she stood a moment to let the sun shine on her face.

A package was in the mailbox, addressed to her, and she opened it, curious. It had no return address. It was a book, *How to Commit Suicide*. The cover showed a picture of Melissa and Colton sitting next to an empty chair, tears streaking their faces. Colton wore a T-shirt that said, "Mama, where are you?" and she peered closely at his face to understand what looked different about him.

He looks older, more grown up, less like the baby I remember and more like a little boy.

The book, although puzzling, incited a different, stronger reaction beyond curiosity. She felt guilt, heavy and weighted guilt, the kind that puts a lump in the pit of your stomach and makes your heart race. Her sweaty palms caused her to drop the book and the packaging, and she ran inside and bolted the door, feeling nauseous. She leaned against the front door, letting it help balance her top-heavy weight and give her trembling legs a break.

Colton. Ah, sweet boy. I miss you too. I'm sorry. I'm so sorry I haven't been there for you. It gets difficult, sometimes, being a grown-up, and maybe someday, I can explain why I haven't been with you. I miss you too. And I miss your mom. And I miss everything we were supposed to do together, and the life we planned to share.

A sharp kick in the ribs sent another wave of guilt through her, and she touched her swollen belly.

Here I am, bringing a child into the world after I all but abandoned the one I became a mama to. What? Will I abandon this little one too? Maybe I'm just not a good person; maybe I'm not mom material; maybe I have no right to keep drawing these little ones to myself. I'm horrible. I'm not mother material.

She was unsure who sent the book, but it had the desired effect— she was rattled. It was too much like what she read in her mom's journal, about the "suicide book" that showed up repeatedly and she couldn't get rid of.

Pulling herself together, she went to her bedroom and retrieved her pistol. If she had it, she knew she'd feel safe. The cold metal felt comforting somehow, and she carried it with her as she went to close the back door that, for some reason, was ajar.

Oh, Dad, you must've left it open when you left this morning.

Then, she made her way to her mother's room, to the closet where the journal was stored. She wanted to read it again, to look for clues about the suicide book her mom wrote about, in case it might help her understand more about the one she received.

Her father's bed was made up tidily, and as she did when she was a little girl, she took a moment to notice the scent and feeling of the cozy bedroom her mother and father shared. There was a mixture of scents—his and hers—that still lingered in the air, even long after her mother's passing. Old Spice and vanilla, shaving cream and hand lotion—the scents of comfort, safety, and home.

Except, something was off. There was a new scent in the room— one she recognized, but couldn't place, and the hair on the back of her neck prickled with nervous energy she couldn't identify the source of. Something wasn't right.

And the door. The closet door. Her mother's closet door wasn't closed; it was ajar, ever so slightly.

She crept toward the closet slowly, her instincts on high alert. She tried to picture the space behind the door, the shelves that were now mostly empty, and the first-aid kit on the floor, the journal on the shelf, but there was something else. She sensed it; she sensed someone lurking just inside and on the other side of the door. She stood quietly, trying to discern whether she heard someone breathing.

I should go get my phone, call John, and wait outside until he comes. Something's not right. Someone is there.

Then, she remembered her gun. And the hang-up calls. And the drive-by car that seemed to pause just outside her house.

She cocked her pistol and inched toward the closet door. She had bought it for this—to defend herself and her child—and John would never make it in time to help her. Her heart pounded in her chest with each step she took, and it took an agonizingly long time to cross the room, past the bed and the bureau, and arrive at the outside of the closet door. She stood behind it, poised with her gun drawn just as she saw cops do in the movies.

With one hand on the gun, she quietly moved her other hand to the doorknob and exhaled slowly. In an instant, she yanked the door open, stepped into the doorframe, and saw a person's shadow. Without hesitation, she fired. Once. Twice. Three times. She fired into the gray depths of the dark closet, and then stopped when she heard a thump.

Someone fell to the floor. Someone was there, just as she suspected.

She turned on the closet light using the long string hanging along the wall just inside the door, her gun still drawn close, in case she might need it again.

On the floor, clutching her own gun, blood pooling around her abdomen, was Melissa.

Savanna rushed to the floor, cradling Melissa's head in what little was left of her lap, and held her lover's head close to her pregnant belly. She felt for a pulse and cried out.

"Melissa? Melissa! What are you doing here? Can you hear me? Melissa!"

Melissa's eyes opened slightly, and she peered into Savanna's face.

"It's true," she said, her voice a mere whisper. "You're. Pregnant."

Savanna squeezed Melissa's hand, and tears welled in her eyes. "You never called. I thought you moved on. I had to move on too. I thought . . . I thought you didn't want me anymore!"

"Always, loved you," Melissa said, her breath becoming shallow. "Hated you for leaving us."

"I'm so sorry! I didn't mean to . . . Why didn't you call? I've missed you . . . I've never stopped wishing . . ."

"Hated you for leaving," Melissa said, long pauses between each word. Then, her eyes closed, and she was gone.

Savanna's tears had no end. She stayed on the closet floor for hours, holding her lover's body, soaking the last bits of warmth from Melissa, rocking back and forth with heart-wrenching moans and sobs of grief. She couldn't speak; she couldn't think; she couldn't move; all she could do was sit there, covered in blood, sobbing at the realization she just killed Melissa and that Melissa, in a rage, came to kill her first.

Gerald found her, hours later, just as her water broke. Nothing is quite as frightening as realizing your grandbaby is about to be born to an inconsolably grieving mother having contractions on the closet floor where her mother and grandmother died, after shooting her ex-lover.

He called for an ambulance first. He called the police department second to report a death. He called John third. "Meet me at the hospital, Savanna's in labor."

John was en route to the hospital when he heard the call over his police scanner.

". . . Deceased female. Homicide department is on the way . . ."

His deputy was on duty, and he knew all would be taken care of from a work standpoint. His child was being born, and he needed to be by Savanna's side. Still, he couldn't help his need to know who died at Savanna and Gerald's house, and more than that, he knew some things shouldn't be picked up by the homicide department to be examined as evidence, such as Mary Ellen's journal.

So, he changed course quickly, and headed for Savanna's house instead, in the opposite direction of the hospital. It wouldn't take him long to grab the journal and be gone again by the time homicide showed up.

When he pulled up at the house, he was glad to see no one had arrived from the police department yet. He moved quickly inside and toward Mary Ellen's closet. The scene that met his eyes was disturbing, even for someone accustomed to seeing death.

What happened here? There were fluids everywhere—mostly blood, but also a pool of soaked carpet made up of something clear. Embryonic fluid?

He looked around the closet quickly, his eyes darting high, low, and all around, looking for Mary Ellen's worn leather journal. Not finding it, he looked in Savanna's room and all over the house. He didn't have much time. He knew Savanna kept the journal in the closet. Why wasn't it there?

He had to leave, he had to get out of the house, and he had to get to Savanna's side. Maybe she took it with her; he would have to ask when she was out of labor. He was certain, though; the journal was gone.

CHAPTER 28

Give Melissa a hug for me, and tell her I love her.

—Savanna

Baby Meg slept, finally, though Savanna didn't know how long her good luck would last. The days with her new daughter were strange ones, long ones, and she hardly knew whether she was coming or going. The nights of waking up every few hours for feedings wore her out, and she never felt rested.

John stayed with her as long as he could after Meg was born, but their new daughter was a secret, so he could not indulge in paternity leave. Gerald was back to work as well, so Savanna was left with a needy two-month-old and the constant whispering of grief. *I wish my mother were here to help me with the baby. I wonder what happened to Colton. How horrible I am that, even in self-defense, I took the life of his mother Melissa. I'm sorry for everything. Melissa. Melissa.*

The mere thought of Melissa was enough to put Savanna in a grief-stricken, guilt-ridden funk for hours. Just as soon as she snapped out of it and remembered she was only protecting herself from an intruder, it was time to feed Meg and settle her in for her next nap. Then, in her quiet time, the thoughts came again, and Melissa's memory haunted her once more.

John said they were going away, that they both needed a fresh start in a place where they didn't have to hide, and they could finally live together as a family. Timing their departure from Cut Bank would be tricky though, he said, and she wasn't exactly sure what he meant by that. But it didn't matter, perhaps; Savanna wasn't even certain moving would solve everything.

John would be there, no matter where they moved, but that was precisely the problem. He was her friend, undoubtedly, and in recent years, he was her lover. But he lacked one key element, and she wasn't sure she could live the rest of her life happily with him as her partner. That is, he wasn't Melissa, and he never would be.

Beyond being tormented by thoughts of John, an aching longing for Melissa, and a new baby who kept her constantly on the edge of sleep deprivation, Savanna was also troubled by the continual arrival of the suicide book. It showed up on her doorstep, in the mailbox, on her car hood, and under the lid of the trashcan in the garage. Every day, she found it somewhere and promptly threw it away, only to have it arrive once more in some unexpected location. It was infuriating, and the face of Colton and Melissa staring back at her was more than she could bear on a good day, let alone on days already filled with grief and sorrow and exhaustion.

As her energy allowed, Savanna searched her house high and low, eagerly looking for her mother's journal that had yet to be located. John said it was missing when he went into the closet after Melissa's death, and her dad hadn't seen it. But she wanted it desperately and believed it was the only thing that could explain more about the suicide book.

In early afternoon, with the sun dipping behind a cloud and cooling things slightly, Savanna placed Meg in her stroller and left the house for a short walk. She waved to her neighbor Casey as she left and, not surprisingly, her feet moved without forethought toward the only place she felt at home anymore—the cemetery and her mother's grave. She was intent on her destination, foggy from too little sleep for too long, so when a black sedan circled the block twice while she pushed the stroller down the sidewalk, she didn't even notice.

Few things escaped Casey's notice though, and she saw that black sedan twice before. Though her cigarette was freshly lit, she extinguished it immediately and went back in the house. She needed to alert that nice detective, Phil Gravy, and tell him what she saw. She hoped she could speak to him, because she knew what happened next—the death van would come, and she didn't want it to.

When Savanna arrived at her mother's grave, she realized she had company. A man stood facing Mary Ellen's headstone, his back to Savanna, and she recognized him immediately. She stood back a pace, respectfully giving him privacy.

"It will all be over soon, Mary Ellen. Don't worry; all will be avenged. It is nearly done," she heard the man say, and hearing his words, she could hold back her intrusion no longer.

"What will be avenged? What is nearly done? Brandon, what did you mean?"

Brandon turned sharply then, his eyes wide with disbelief at seeing Savanna there, and he sputtered and fumbled for a response.

"It's nothing. It's just . . . Well . . . What I meant was . . . a few of us—John, your dad, and I—we're really close to finding your mom's journal. Yeah, that's it. Uh, and I know that will be something you'll be glad to have back again." Brandon fumbled in his pockets, shifted his weight back and forth, and then changed the subject. "How's Meg? I love her name, by the way. For Mary Ellen and Gerald. Very sweet. You doing OK?"

Savanna nodded, accustomed by now to saying she was doing well when she really wasn't. The falsehood came so easily these days. Her life was a muddled mess, but there was no point in sharing that until she got some things figured out for herself. Did she love John? Did she see herself being his wife forever? If they left town, what would happen to her dad? How could he cope without her and her mom? It hardly seemed fair to him, but how could she stay in this town now?

"Just fine, Brandon. A little sleepy, but babies will do that to you. I'm glad to see Mom having some company. It's nice of you to visit her."

"It's the least I can do, and I miss her," he replied. "Come by the coffee shop sometime. I'll hook you up with a cuppa liquid energy, OK?"

"I will," she promised and managed a weak smile of reassurance as she watched him walk away. In that moment, despair sunk her to new lows. She didn't want to figure things out, she didn't want to go by the coffee shop, and she was so, so tired. She just wanted to go, to escape, to be done with this mess. She made her decision immediately. She proceeded to her mother's grave then for her visit, to introduce Meg and to say what she came to say.

"I miss you, Mom. I look forward to seeing you again soon. Give Melissa a hug for me, and tell her I love her."

CHAPTER 29

It's a strange situation we find ourselves in, but at the end of the day, we are all here to protect the citizens of Cut Bank, even if that means protecting them from one of our own.

—John

Tonight, John, the e-mail said. *I need you on call tonight.* John replied immediately from his smartphone: *You got it, boss. I'll be awaiting your call.*

Then, he ducked out of the office and walked briskly down the street to the park. Tucked among city buildings, the small park had a gazebo and a small playground next to a pond hijacked year-round by ducks and geese. He surveyed his options. The gazebo might be bugged, but the swing set probably wouldn't be.

It might have looked strange to a passerby to see a cop swinging on the swing set midday, but by that point, John couldn't care less about appearances. From his trouser pocket, he withdrew a disposable cell phone and quickly dialed the number the Midnight Caller insisted he memorize and never write down. His call was answered immediately.

"Tonight," John said simply.

"Understood. I suspected as much. We're all ready; all the pieces are set," the Midnight Caller replied.

"Thanks for everything," John said. "I can't wait to have this behind us."

"There's work to be done before that can happen. Stay focused."

And the line went dead.

4:08 P.M.

Fourteen months to the day after Mary Ellen's death, Savanna arrived home with Meg sleeping in the stroller after visiting her mom's grave. She woke up Meg long enough to change her diaper and feed her, and then rocked her back to sleep.

As she laid Meg in the crib that was hers as a baby, Savanna planted a long, lingering kiss on her daughter's head. She wiped away a tear rolling down her cheek.

4:20 P.M.

Fourteen months to the day after his wife's death, Gerald pulled up at the country club and parked his car. He rolled down the window to get some air and wiped away a tear rolling down his cheek. Just as the Midnight Caller told him to expect, a spa technician walked up to his car and handed him a package.

"These run back for the last three months. I adjusted the microphone recently, so the recordings from inside the sauna last night and earlier this week are crystal clear," the young woman said. Gerald handed the woman an envelope of crisp bills and thanked her.

He then drove toward home, but didn't stop at his house. Instead, as he was instructed, he turned the corner, entered a back alley, and parked his car behind Casey's house.

4:47 P.M.

Casey found it easier now to reach Phil Gravy. Unlike the two previous times, years ago, when she saw the black sedan, she no longer needed to call the police station to reach him. Instead, she simply walked back to her spare bedroom and knocked. Having a detective live with you was awesome, she thought. He paid her a little money to keep his residence in her spare room quiet, which was enough to help her with cigarettes, dog bones, and a steak on Friday nights. An old woman didn't need much more than those small comforts.

She knocked on the bedroom door. "Detective Gravy? You in there?" She didn't know why he wouldn't be, especially since he hadn't left her house in more than a year.

Sure enough, he was there. "Come in."

As she entered, he said, "And you can just call me Phil, OK? Remember, I'm not a detective anymore, not really. Did you need something?"

"Yes, I need to tell you I saw the black sedan again. That's thirteen times now. The death van will be next, just as it always is."

"Thank you, Casey. I have some friends coming over tonight, so can you let them in when they arrive?"

"Yes, Detective. I'll keep counting the trips the black sedan makes around the block. Will that be helpful?"

"Yes, thank you again."

5:15 P.M.

Brandon walked into Dr. Spence's office a few minutes early for his 5:30 appointment. Dr. Spence looked up from his desk, surprised. "You're early, son. Oh, no matter. It was just a prescription refill you needed, wasn't it?" Dr. Spence asked.

"Yes, just a refill script. And one other thing. I need you to stand up and walk slowly toward the closet. Don't make a sound, or you'll force me to use this," he said, pointing a pistol directly at the doctor's heart.

Dr. Spence, caught off guard, did exactly as he was told. Bound and gagged, he was left in his office closet, and Brandon made sure to lock it before leaving the office.

5:30 P.M.

Savanna walked to the kitchen table with a pad of paper and a pen. She began to write:

Dear John, I'm sorry I can't stay. Please take care of little Meggy, and know that I love you. There's some place else I need to be right now . . .

5:35 P.M.

Governor Jeffries picked up the phone midway through the first ring. "Yes?"

"Mayor Travis is on his way, sir," his secretary Christine said.

"Send him right in, and we do not wish to be disturbed in any way."

"Yes, sir."

Hanging up the phone, Governor Jeffries turned back to his desk to resume his conversation with his guest. "The mayor is on his way. It's show time."

"Yep, we're ready, Governor," the chief of the State Patrol said and turned to alert his deputies to be ready to arrest the man who walked through the office door next.

6:10 P.M.

The sky was beginning to darken when Gerald and Brandon walked into the guest room of Casey's home, though it looked less like a guest room now and more like Command Central.

Phil rose from his desk behind several computer monitors to greet the men with warm handshakes. "It's wonderful to see you both again," he said.

"Definitely, Phil. Thanks for all your help," Gerald said. "It's quite a setup you have here."

Phil sat down again, motioning the men to sit on folding chairs across from him. "That it is; that it is," he said, gesturing to the equipment surrounding him. "It hasn't been easy piecing this whole thing together, but somehow we pulled it off, didn't we?"

"Yes, we did," Brandon said. "I'm still amazed at how you figured this whole thing out."

"It hasn't been easy, but I couldn't have done it without you and Gerald and John. I mean, I've had this whole town bugged since the week after Mary Ellen passed away, but the Mayor and his cronies needed to think I was in Mexico, so having legs in this town has been difficult. And as I said, without you three, I could not have done it."

"The Midnight Caller thing was top-notch brilliance, Phil," said Gerald.

"Without it, I don't see how we could even be here in this spot tonight. I needed your help, but if you had known who I was all along, I'm afraid we could not have pulled this whole thing off," Phil said. "Brandon would have had a difficult time appearing to the Mayor as if he knew nothing, though, all the while knowing I was still in the picture; John needed to be on a need-to-know basis as well, with Mark so close by; and Gerald, you likely would have had me arrested if you'd known it was me calling you."

"Arrested?" Brandon asked. "Why?"

Phil and Gerald exchanged knowing glances. "Mary Ellen's life insurance money," Phil said. "I swindled it away from Gerald years ago, back before she died. But when I realized what crooks we have in Cut Bank—the Mayor, Mark Crew, and Dr. Spence—I had a change of heart. I used Mary Ellen's money to launch this investigation, to get to the bottom of what's been going on in Cut Bank for years—crooked politics, murders disguised as suicides, and swindling the people of Cut Bank out of their right to a democratic, aboveboard local government. Tonight, we set things right, once and for all."

"Here's to that," Gerald said, raising an imaginary beer bottle. A celebratory drink would have to wait, for now. "And I meant what I said, Phil. I consider this investigation money well spent, and I do not intend to press charges against you, ever, for pilfering Mary Ellen's life insurance. You turned out all right, Phil. Just keep my baby girl safe tonight and my granddaughter, and we'll call it even."

Phil nodded. "It would be an honor. Ready to wrap this up? We have Dr. Spence locked up, and the State Patrol will move in shortly to retrieve him and arrest him. We have the Mayor under arrest, probably at this very moment, in the Governor's mansion. And we have Mark Crew circling the block in a black sedan. Savanna's safe at home, and I have cameras all over your house, Gerald. We're ready for John to do his thing now."

7:30 P.M.

"Gentlemen, it's time," said John to a standing circle of police officers. "It's a strange situation we find ourselves in, but at the end of the day, we are all here to protect the citizens of Cut Bank, even if that means protecting them from one of our own. Our orders come straight from the Governor's office, and we have the State Patrol as backup. We have ample, prevailing reason to believe two of our citizens, Savanna and her newborn daughter Meg, are in danger of becoming homicide victims . . . at the hands of Mark Crew.

"Instead of relying on you to go in afterward to clean up his mess, as many of you have done for him before, I rely on you tonight to go in and stop this crime from happening.

"At 8:00 P.M., we'll be on location, ready to catch our police chief red-handed, and making an arrest."

7:45 P.M.

"The police officers are on their way, the sedan is circling, and movement detectors inside the house say Savanna is in the kitchen and still very much alive," Phil said.

Gerald and Brandon watched the computer monitors, sitting on the edge of their seats, and noticeably nervous.

7:50 P.M.

Savanna looked out the window and noticed a car pulling up in front of her house. It was the one she saw circling most of the evening, and she wondered who might be inside.

It won't matter much longer anyway, she thought.

Moving toward her mother's closet, she took a last, long glance at the living room. She placed several notes on the coffee table, each with a name on them—Dad, John, Meg.

7:59 P.M.

The patio door opened, and underneath a black mask, Mark Crew smiled. He was here before, and not much had changed. He started to move toward the back of the house, toward the closet where he would wait for Savanna, hangman's rope in hand, but he didn't make it far.

The front door was smashed in, and four police officers stormed into the house, weapons drawn, yelling, "Drop your weapon; you're under arrest!"

Mark put his hands in the air and sank to his knees.

8:01 P.M.

John pushed his way into the house, past the police officers. Seeing that the Chief was secured and not endangered, he walked quickly through the house, calling for Savanna.

Meg awoke from her nap, yawning, and John heard her crying in her crib. He went to her and picked her up, crooning in her ear.

8:02 P.M.

Savanna took her last breath. The noose around her neck held her vertically, swinging from the hook at the top of her mother's closet. Her grandmother died here, so did her mother, and so did her lover. Now, it was her turn to reunite with them. As her heart stopped, she saw Melissa's face and knew all was forgiven. They would be together again soon.

John found her a moment later, but she was already gone. He rushed into the living room, calling to his men to get an ambulance to the house, and his eyes landed on the folded sheets of paper on the coffee table. He grabbed the stack of notes and ran with Meg across the street, back through the alley to the back door, and into the guest room of Casey's home.

8:10 P.M.

Gerald and John wept, clutching Meg between them. Savanna's notes were read and destroyed, removing all evidence that her death was suicide.

"Hold Meggy," John said. "I need to go back across the street and get this scene documented. We couldn't prove Mark's involvement with Mary Ellen's death or her mother's death, but the least we can do is pin this unexpected tragedy on someone who will make an excellent scapegoat. Mark's time is up. He's going away for a long, long time."

Something felt so right to John about documenting Savanna's death as a homicide. Tears fell as he wrote out his crime scene documentation, but it was the right thing to do—for Mary Ellen and Sue, for his first wife, and for the woman who would have been his second wife. The reign of Cut Bank's egomaniacs was over, finally.

Across the street, Phil put an arm around Casey and said, "Your brother, the Governor, will be proud of you. If you hadn't found me and told me about the black sedan and the death van, as you call it, we never would have gotten to the bottom of this."

Casey shrugged. "They were nice ladies, all of them." She didn't know what else to say, so she waved casually to the men gathered in her guest room and said, "I'm going out for a cigarette."

EPILOGUE

John relaxed in the sun, his children beside him. His job as the new chief of police was challenging and time consuming, but fulfilling at the same time. When he could get away for a vacation with his little family, he felt grateful.

Nearby, Gerald picked up a beach ball and shouted to his grandkids. "Who wants to play?" he asked, and all three kids followed him into the waves.

John's cell phone rang, and even though he was on vacation, he answered it. It was the right thing to do.

"John, it's Phil."

"How are you, Mayor? Everything going all right?"

"Just fine, yes. Wanted to let you know Council met last night, and I can fill you in on the minor details later. But I thought you would want to know the voters turned out in record number to approve a bond measure for erecting a park in Mary Ellen's honor. They really liked the plans we drew up for the ballot. Little People Memorial Park is a go, and the attached arboretum dedicated to Sue and Savanna passed. Thanks for all your support."

"That's great news; I'm really pleased to hear it. And Brandon's rezoning request? For the bar? Did that pass?"

"He withdrew it, actually. He had a change of plans, it seems. He's taking his brewery money and investing it in something different, instead. It's sort of a mixed-use place for local kids. He'll have after-school care, tutoring, and support for foster kids and their families. He's calling it "ME Zone," and the schools are already really excited about it."

"ME Zone? That's kind of different," John said.

"Mary Ellen's initials. He's dedicating his project to her. I think she'd be proud, don't you?"

"I do," John said.

"Well, see you when you get back, I guess," Phil said. "Have a great rest of your trip."

"I sure will. And don't forget, adoption day is on the 15th, right after we get back. Will you be there to support Colton and me? It's a big day for us all—Lucy and Meg are getting a brother, and Colton is getting a daddy."

"I wouldn't miss it for the world," Phil said.

John clicked off the call and sat watching his children with their grandfather. The way Gerald took to all three of his kids—Lucy, Meg, and Colton—amazed him, and he couldn't wait to get home and resume his crazy, happy life in Cut Bank.

ABOUT THE AUTHOR

Elvis Slaughter is an educator, consultant, publisher, writer and criminologist. He's written and published nonfiction books since 2005, which include *The Ghost of Hollandale, The American Genocide, The Malcolm X Project, Epiphany Or Sin,* and *Safer Jail And Prison Matters,* and he's co-authored *Uncle Percy's Blessings* with his daughter, Dr. Loni Slaughter. The suspense thriller *Egomaniac* is Elvis' first fiction offering and has set the tone for future similar projects. *Egomaniac* has exceeded Elvis' expectation in reviews, acceptance, and ratings. Elvis also volunteers his time to community work and is involved in public speaking. Elvis is devoted to mentoring the next generation of leaders, and he loves exploring Chicago's vibrant jazz scene during his free time.